The Abbey View

Louise Richmond

Thank you for reading my debut novel

with love

Louise

x

find me on instagram —

louise_richmond_authour

Chapter One

Conor woke. It was a winter morning and still dark. He picked up his phone to check the time. He guessed before looking. *6.40 am*, he said to himself. Then he looked down at his phone. He smiled a little, satisfied with himself that he was so close. It was 6.42. He was good at this little game of guess the time, always within ten minutes.

Conor got up at the same time every working day, which was every day apart from his one day off a week. His alarm was due to buzz at 6.45. He snuggled back into his blankets, cosy and warm, and smiled. Three more whole minutes, he thought. What bliss. The minutes passed, and his alarm went off. He got up straight away. No snoozing.

He had prepared his uniform for work the night before, and his light blue manager's work shirt and black suit were clean and pressed and hanging from the door frame, ready to go. His shoes were neatly polished and on the doormat. He even had his favourite breakfast cereal, pineapple granola, and a bowl set out on the table. Talk about organised. That is why he made a good manager: his attention to detail and his organisational skills.

Conor took a quick shower, dressed and then had his pineapple granola and a mug of coffee. He put his bowl and cup in the dishwasher and wiped the table. After putting on his perfectly polished shoes, he grabbed his black winter coat with the thermal lining and fluffy hood from the hooks by the door and headed to work.

Conor enjoyed his twenty-minute walk to work, even on a cool, crisp winter morning like this one. It left him feeling awake and invigorated, ready for the day. The route takes him past the magnificent ruins of a Cistercian abbey, standing at the edge of a small lake. *Beautiful*, thought Conor as he breathed in the cold air. He felt a connection to the building, imagining its past inhabitants and the spiritual nature of their existence there. The lake itself was picturesque, but the two together were something else. It always made him smile as he passed by.

He never tired of the view or became immune to it. Every day, he appreciated its place on the landscape. He had the best work commute anyone could wish for and was eternally grateful for it. No getting stuck in lines of traffic. Just fresh air and beautiful views, whatever the weather. He had a real sense of satisfaction with his life, and he told himself so every morning: *It was going to be another great day.*

The abbey was founded circa AD 1152. The Cistercian monks displaced the hermits that occupied the area, some of whom joined the abbey and the rest being paid to move on.

The Cistercians were famous for closely following the rules, for their desire to separate themselves from society, their austerity, and community spirit. They were careful about who they allowed to enter their abbeys. Besides building a wall around the monastery and posting monks to watch the gate, they situated their abbeys away from large settlements.

The monks did not eat for at least nine hours after waking. In summer, they ate only lunch and a light supper, reduced to just one meal in winter. The Cistercian way of life did not allow monks to live in comfort but provided just enough to keep a monk sustained for his duties.

The lay brothers, the monks from poorer backgrounds, were responsible for all the manual and agricultural work on the abbey's land. The lay brothers slept in the cellarium, or storehouse, on straw mattresses on the floor.

Sometimes, they would sleep out in the fields with their sheep.

The choir monks were ordained as priests. They would descend the night stairs in white robes at 2 am for the first mass of the day and don their vestments.

***

James Bridge was a small town popular with tourists. Families came for days out to have picnics at the lake during the spring and summer months, even in the autumn, but Conor had not yet seen anyone having a winter picnic, though he thought it would still be a lovely spot if you wrapped up warm. Coachloads on historical tours of the area would visit the abbey all year round, but of course, it was busiest in summer.

The Abbey View, a bar restaurant serving food all day, was a firm favourite with both the locals and the tourists. Conor had always enjoyed working there. He had started as a casual bar worker and had progressed to manager, a position he was delighted to hold. His family were so proud of him.

He enjoyed having had the opportunity to meet so many different people over the years. A lot of the tourists that visited James Bridge would return year after year. Others would come once and never be seen again. Still, he enjoyed meeting each of them, the lovely variety of accents he would hear, telling him where they had travelled from, who their travel companions were, and where they were visiting next. It was like he was going on the adventure with them, making every day different. It was nice to see people enjoying their visit to his town.

The locals were equally as charming, happy to entertain visitors with tales of the Cistercians and the folklore of the abbey — they did not let the truth get in the way of a good story. It entertained themselves as much as the visitors, regaling their tall tales.

One such tale was told by Sean, a local for many years but originally from Ireland, and a regular of the Abbey View.

Sean always sat on the wooden stool at the bar, drinking his usual pint of Guinness. He sat in the dimly lit corner just out of the busiest part of the bar but near enough to hear and join in all the conversations. He and Conor loved a good old chat on a quieter evening in the bar.

Sean's "Headless Monk" tale was a favourite with the tourists. Tonight, there was a coach trip in, and Sean was ready to entertain them.

And so, he began:

"The traditional history of the abbey that you will have heard today on your visit is that of the Cistercian Order of monks that lived here in James Bridge and inhabited the abbey. Now, there are lesser-known stories of the monks who lived here as the abbey began its dissolution and decay.

"Erosion is not spontaneous; it took hundreds of years for the abbey ruins to appear as they do today. And the spirit of the abbey and the people that lived here take generations to crumble away, if they ever do.

"There was once a monk ordained as a priest who slept in a room at the top of the winding stone night stairs. His sleep was often filled with visions, messages from God, he called them. They often made little sense to him, but he believed, nonetheless.

"His day began at 2 am. He descended the night stairs and dressed in his vestments, which covered his clothing. He found this early hour of the new day a spiritual hour to be up. He was dedicated to his role and had resided in the abbey for many years.

"The monks befell a cruel fate as the suppression approached. One morning, in darkness, he descended the night stairs, ready to declare his unfaltering faith. There was a thunderstorm, the loudest and most powerful he could ever recall.

"Peering through the small, slit window as he descended the stairs, he could see that the lightning was illuminating the whole of the night sky as if it were day just for a moment. He could see the sheep on the hills, and then blackness returned. What a sight. The thunder roared above. He was awed at the orchestra of the thunderstorm as the lightning danced along. But then, it was as if he had become possessed.

"An evil presence took over his soul. He took to the abbey kitchen and retrieved a cleaver intended for preparing meat. In a sleep-like trance, he entered the lay-brothers' dorm. They were still sleeping soundly. In a rage, the priest beheaded every monk — severed heads and blood everywhere.

"The lightning struck, and the thunder roared. The devil possessing him left, and he looked upon a bloody scene of horror. In seeing what he had done, he took the cleaver and killed himself."

Silence.

Sean always left a dramatic pause …

"It is rumoured that the monks' unhappy souls never left the abbey as they had died in such a tragic way, and whenever there is a thunderstorm here in James Bridge, the headless monks can be seen wandering the abbey grounds. You never know when someone might unexpectedly turn into … a murderer."

He finishes with:

"It's only a tale, mind, and there are no thunderstorms forecast for tonight."

The tourists gasp, and then laughing erupts, sometimes a round of applause followed by "Can I get you a drink, Sean?"

The tourists love him. His Irish accent adds to his storytelling charm.

Conor did not believe a word of Sean's tales but enjoyed them all the same, seeing the entertainment they brought to the patrons. And their gasps, the giggles and the fun. He had no idea how he came up with such gruesome tales.

Conor poured the drinks for all the happy customers. He laughed, too, even though he had heard the tale hundreds of times before. Conor had always felt proud to be the manager of Abbey View, a place where strangers could talk like old friends. Where stories were shared, and fun could be had by all. It was a great atmosphere. He worked hard and had always been content to be there.

Conor had moved to James Bridge from County Laois in Ireland. This is why he enjoyed hearing Sean's accent telling tales at the bar, as it reminded him of home. Conor had left Ireland at eighteen to study music at a university in England, not far for James Bridge, and eventually, this is where he settled.

He had a comfortable two-bed groundfloor apartment with beautiful views from the rear, overlooking an alpaca farm. In the distance, he could see the alpacas frolicking in the field. He especially loved this view when the baby alpacas, or crias as he discovered they were called, arrived in the late spring.

Conor came from a close-knit and loving family. He was especially close to his younger sister Marie, but he always felt something was waiting for him out there in the big wide world, a part of himself to discover.

His passion was music. He could play a range of instruments: the piano, the guitar and his favourite instrument, the Irish bodhrán drum. He took his bodhrán drum everywhere. It was the one his mammy and daddy had bought him back home in Ireland before he left on his big adventure to England.

***

It was Saturday night at the Abbey View, and Conor had brought his drum to play with a couple of other locals — not an official gig but a regular singalong that everyone could join. There was Sammy on her viola, Derrick on the tin whistle and Aneesha playing her flute. He knew Aneesha from university. They had always played together back in their student days, and then, quite by chance, had bumped into one another at the Abbey View one evening, and the regular singalongs started.

It was common in pubs back home in Ireland to have a singalong, but not so much here in England, he had discovered. Not an impromptu one, anyway, just the locals doing it for fun. Conor had never understood why, as everyone seemed to enjoy it, and the musicians would get a free pint or two out of it.

Derrick joined next. He had retired to James Bridge, and he played the harmonica and the tin whistle but he always said the tin whistle was a better fit with the bodhrán. Then, one evening, Sammy introduced herself to the trio. She played the viola. Conor invited her to join: the bodhrán drum, the flute, the tin whistle and the viola — what a sound when they all played together.

The best part was that this sort of band had no lead singer or set playlist. Everyone joined in. Clapping, stamping feet, hollering if they didn't know the words. It was an uplifting and unique experience for all the visitors to James Bridge. Even the coach guides, who also enjoyed an evening in the Abbey View, had listed it as one of the top things to do in James Bridge. *Visit the Abbey View for the food and a musical treat*, they would tell the passengers.

In these cold winter months, the fire was ablaze, the music would play, drinks were poured, and the visitors would say it was a great time of year to visit.

Tonight, the Abbey View looked very festive, with an eight-foot Christmas tree standing floor to ceiling, adorned with the most unique ornaments, handmade by the local shopkeepers and craftworkers.

Conor had two favourite decorations; his first, the glass baubles with waves of colour running through them: festive greens, golds and reds made by Sophia, who owned a studio not far from the abbey, where visitors could go and watch the glass being blown. Sophia also made the smaller hanging glass decorations with images of deer and robins, which she made in her kiln.

The second and the more unusual choice, but equally as beautiful and impressive, were the hanging iron keys made by the local blacksmith, Bobby. Conor had watched Bobby in his workshop; the iron sparks flying as he hammered the orange glowing metal over the fire.

Conor stood behind a Perspex screen with the other visitors for his own health and safety, but Bobby himself was bare-chested, so hot from the intensity of the fire and the physical labour. Conor was relieved that Bobby at least wore an apron, although he could see burns and scars on his arms. The keys looked like they could open enormous gates to magical kingdoms or secret gardens. Not flimsy, but big and chunky, strung with ribbon, and the children were told these were Santa's magic keys that could open any lock.

The fairy lights on the tree were golden and twinkled as if they were following the rhythms of the music. Conor held his bodhrán drum in his left hand — quite large to hold with one hand — and beat it with the two-sided drumstick he had in his right hand. It moved so fast; it was such a skill.

As it was nearly Christmas, they played a few songs to celebrate the season, some of their favourites, and requests taken from the other patrons — the aromas of the fire and the spiced mulled wine added to the festive feel of the evening.

When Conor had finished playing, Bobby approached him with a small gift wrapped in brown parcel paper with a blue ribbon attached and a small white rectangular gift tag. "Merry Christmas," he said, handing the small package to Conor, winking at him and walking away again.

Conor called after him, "Merry Christmas, Bobby. Thanks a million."

He put the small parcel in his jacket pocket while he packed his drum and chatted away with his fellow musicians. Conor was working over the festive period, so he wouldn't see his family again this year, but he wanted to be here at the Abbey View to ensure everything ran smoothly. It was not overly busy at this time of year, but a pub in a town that draws in both locals and tourists all year round is always busy enough, and as manager, he took pride in everything running well.

A specialist coach trip was booked in on Christmas Day—festive historical tours. Conor worked closely with the tour group companies when they were putting packages together. He had already discussed the menu with the chef and ordered his own meal to enjoy later in the day after he had finished work.

Later, when Conor got home, he felt for his house keys in his coat pocket, pulled them out and the little gift. He opened the door, stepped inside, and locked the door behind him.

He hung his coat on the hooks by the entrance and placed the gift on the table, looking around the bare room—he did not have a Christmas tree or any decorations. He took a glass from the cupboard, turned on the tap, filled it, then sat at the table, taking a drink and placing it down while he picked up his present. How nice, he thought. He was used to receiving a drink or two when playing at the Abbey View, but no one had ever bought him a gift. He decided to open the package and not save it for Christmas Day.

He read the tag. *To open doors ~ B.* Conor untied the blue ribbon and removed the brown parcel paper. Now, he was holding a small white rectangular box. He opened the lid. Inside was one of Bobby's iron keys.

This one was long and heavy. It had four prongs at the top and a round, ball-shaped end. He had never seen anything like it before. It had a marking down the long edge that looked like the two interlocking circles from the diagrams he had learnt about in mathematics at school. He wondered if it opened anything, then concluded it was just ornamental like the keys on the Christmas tree at Abbey View. *Thanks,*

15

Bobby, he said to himself and popped it back into his jacket pocket for safekeeping.

Chapter Two

In and out, in and out of the stone arches, the waxing moon in the sky above, calling every molecule in Conor's body to action. In and out, his skin bubbling. His nervous system fully wired, his heart flip-flopping. Hands shaking. So lost in the physical sensations within his body, he had momentarily forgotten where he was. He was unable to focus on his majestic surroundings, the ruins of a Cistercian abbey — one of the best-preserved Cistercian monasteries in England.

Founded over 860 years ago, the Grade I listed monument was a marvel to behold. One of many beautiful abbeys in Yorkshire. The dramatic outline towered up to the moon as though crying out from a past long distant but not wholly gone, somehow still present there in the existing remains. The abbey's arches, its thick stone walls, its form and shape transformed in the moonlight as the ruins cast shadows and reflected onto the lake at its foot.

The lake, fed by a nearby river, was smooth, frozen at the edges, mirroring the abbey and the waxing moon that would, in a couple of nights, become the winter's cold full moon. December and winter were beginning for the people of the Northern Hemisphere.

The Old English and Anglo-Saxon names are the Moon Before Yule or the Long Night Moon, referring to the longest night of the year in the Northern Hemisphere: the winter solstice.

Conor's breathing was rapid and shallow, a misty cloud in the cold air. His fingertips tingled. His jaw clenched, teeth tight together. His shoulders were so high and stiff that his head tilted and stuck to one side with the tension. His heart still flip-flopping, like it was trying desperately to find its rhythm. His vision fussy and blurred as the anxiety raced up from his toes into the back of his head and to the ends of each of his fingers. Adrenaline flooded every inch of his body. He was having an anxiety attack. Real-time had stopped. Now, his irregular heartbeat was trying to keep to its own tempo of the passing of time, like some strange internal clock that didn't know whether to tick backwards or forwards. Real-time was no longer a concept that existed for him. He had no idea how long he had been here at the abbey.

Eventually, his internal system ran out of steam. And, as it did, time returned to Conor's reality. Suddenly, he could feel the coldness of the frosty stones of the archway as he leaned against it for support, propped up as his energy drained.

He had stopped his weaving walk through the arches. He saw the moon. He stared at it for a few minutes as he finally caught hold of a full breath in. It was a waxing gibbous moon tonight, not quite full, a sign for Conor from the universe, perhaps: the moon phase that calls for reflection, a time to look back on life lessons and the internal growth that has come from them and, most importantly, for Conor to use this reflection to adjust his current goals and life path accordingly.

Finally, as if taking back control and ownership of his body, Conor moved himself over to the grassy belt that surrounded the abbey. He sat on the cold, wet grass, allowing his hands to roam over and between the soft blades and took another breath.

Then, he suddenly realised he could feel the prickly, cold, wet, frosted grass on his feet and between his toes. Why was he out at night at the start of winter with no socks or shoes? As this physical sensation of the grass on his feet returned, he looked down towards them. He paused for just a moment, then, as if his brain had fully switched back on, it received the engram memory image of the absence of his shoes and socks.

Time to walk home, Conor said to himself. He rose to his feet, observing them again. It was a ten-minute walk home in his bare feet. What if he were spotted by people leaving their Christmas parties and making their way home? So, he began creating a story as to why he had bare feet. It needed to be believable in case he should get funny looks or, worse still, meet someone from work. He began the short walk, which, without his shoes and socks and the embarrassment he felt, may as well have been one hundred miles.

The first story: *Well, I decided to go for a late-night paddle in the lake and misplaced my shoes and socks. I know, how silly of me*, he practised. No, he thought, that's not at all believable. Why would anyone be paddling on such a cold, dark evening?

His toes were now so cold they were turning blue and were losing feeling. What is believable?! He racked his brain. *I really hope I don't see a soul.*

He tried out another story: *Well, you see, I was out walking, and I stood in a wet, icy puddle with both feet and got my shoes and socks wet. I took them off to wring dry, but a dog ran off with my shoes.* And my socks, or not? Which is more believable and, if not my socks, where are my socks now? I lost them in the dark? Maybe another dog took those. Or a barn owl swooped down and thought they were a mouse.

He continued to walk while trying to find the right story. No, no, that's not right either, he thought. Why would anyone with any shred of sanity think that was true? It would be so much easier if I could just be completely honest.

It didn't matter in the end, as he had arrived home without seeing anyone or anyone seeing him. He did not need a story after all. He did not need to make himself a liar or make himself look completely stupid. Relief.

***

It was Thursday, which meant music night at the Abbey View. Sean was looking forward to an entertaining evening and a pint. The Celtic music Conor and the rest of the band played reminded Sean of his home town. Conor always gave him a free pint and sometimes bought him a meal when he knew he was short on cash.

Conor had already worked one shift and enjoyed a peaceful break at the abbey. He found a quiet spot sheltered from the wind and the rain and enjoyed being outside for a while. The cold breeze had invigorated him for his second shift of the day.

During the winter, there were no casual bar staff, so Conor covered an extra shift or two. He didn't mind especially, but he wouldn't be able to play with the band this evening. Back at the Abbey View, Conor checked on the staff and customers, ensuring everything had run smoothly in his short absence. All was fine.

Aneesha and Sammy arrived together.

"Good evening," smiled Conor. "The usual?"

"Evening, Conor," said Aneesha. "Yes, please."

Sammy nodded in agreement. "Please," she said, placing her viola case on top of the bar.

Ten minutes later, Derrick arrived. "Good evening all," he said cheerfully.

"Listen, I'm working tonight, and we're short-staffed, so I won't be able to play," said Conor.

"Aw, that's a shame. We'll miss you," said Aneesha, unpacking her flute.

"You're working too hard," said Derrick.

"The usual?" Conor asks him.

"Aye, yes," he said, "and maybe …"

"… a packet of salt and vinegar crisps." Conor finished his sentence, already knowing what he was going to say.

Conor continued serving the customers, and a while later, heard the music start.

"Yes, what can I get for you?" he asked the next customer, smiling and singing along.

Sean had his usual spot at the far end of the bar. He was enjoying his pint of Guinness until he was distracted by the bodhrán drum. Or rather the lack of it. He looked up to check, as if not believing his ears, until his eyes confirmed that Conor was not playing. He spotted Conor behind the bar. It was not unusual for one of the musicians not to play; it was, after all, a voluntary affair, but Sean's favourite instrument in the band was the bodhrán drum. He could not recall a time when Conor had not played with the rest of the band.

***

Conor was wandering the abbey. He had been missing home recently, and he felt a connection here. It reminded him of the ruined castle he played in as a boy. Dunstan Castle was near his school playing field — just sitting there. Like the football posts, the swings and the slide, it was a part of his childhood playground, and the greatest place to play hide-and-seek. He would play for hours, until it was time to go home for supper.

Conor felt stressed and anxious like he had lost himself somehow. At what point had this happened, he questioned himself.

Eventually, he walked home and went straight to bed. He did not even have the energy to brush his teeth or change his clothes. He locked the door, went to his bedroom, removed his shoes and crawled into bed. He lay there, his mind so busy, looking for answers. He was exhausted but didn't want to sleep until he had searched every dark, dusty corner of his brain for the reason he felt so low and then find a solution. He couldn't face another day without something changing.

His mind ran through the day, looking for clues, thinking about what had and had not gone well. What had and had not made him happy. He worried about the impression he was giving of himself to people. He wanted people to like him, and people did like him, but now he was questioning everything. Not sure who he was anymore or what he enjoyed doing in his leisure time, because he never had any. He did not know what made him happy; he was always so tired. He didn't understand what was making him sad. It was like there was a disconnect between two different versions of himself.

He cried big tears. He could not find the answers, and it was getting late. What could he do to pull himself out of this unhappiness? His head hurt from all the thinking. He clenched his teeth together so tightly his mouth hurt. His body felt alien like it did not even belong to him. Or maybe it was these thoughts that were alien. He stared at the ceiling, internally crying out *help me, please, someone help me.*

He had seen advertisements about talking out if you were suffering from mental health or low moods, but what words do you say, and what can anyone do? He had once tried talking to a colleague. *Yeah, mate, we all feel a bit tired and a bit low at some time or another, but you just need to get on with it. You have nothing to be sad about. You have a good job, a supportive family, a nice place to live.* Well, that had made him feel like crap for saying anything, so he had tried to ignore that part of himself. Push it down, way down. Ignore it.

He had done the total opposite of what he should have done. He had pushed it down in the dark depths to fester inside, instead of bringing it out into the light where he could deal with it. And now, it was making noise. Lots of noise. To be heard. That part of him that needed to be seen, validated, believed.

He never wanted to be seen as unappreciative of his life or complaining when he knew of other people going through tough times. So, he was pushing his feelings down further. But now, they were rising from under the surface of his skin like it was a full moon, and he was a werewolf that had been hiding his wolf secret and had learned how to suppress it. But he could no longer deny that part of himself. The wolf was emerging.

He was looking for kindness in other people, which he couldn't find. He saw people being kind; he saw kindness in others, but he did not know how to receive it. He wanted help, but he did not know how to obtain it. It seemed like some elusive entity, always out of his grasp.

***

Conor worked more double shifts all that week. He was tired. As he put the key in the door and turned it to lock up the Abbey View, he thought *another day and night shift done.* He saw a snowflake land on the sleeve of his black winter coat. He looked up at the street light and saw it was indeed snowing—falling slowly and silently to the ground. A dusting lay on the street like the icing sugar his chef sprinkled on the chocolate log earlier. He took a few steps, then turned his head back to look at his footprints in the virgin snow. Now it really should feel like Christmastime, but it did not.

As he approached the abbey, the clouds parted just enough to glimpse the full moon.

Then, something else caught his eye — a shadow moving in the abbey cloister. He wondered who would be at the abbey at this time of night. He didn't usually see anyone on his way home after a night shift.

As Conor got closer, he realised it was Sean. Conor felt a shiver; it could have been the cold, but it was like he had felt a connection to Sean for a moment, and he knew something was not quite right. He had to check everything was okay before he continued home.

"Sean," Conor called out as he approached him. After no response, he called out again. "Sean!"

Sean turned and faced him this time.

"Everything okay, mate?" Conor asked.

For a moment, Sean was silent, his mouth moving as though he wanted to speak but couldn't. Conor moved closer to him to check he wasn't hurt — a bump to the head or something. He looked closely at his friend. He seemed okay, so he tried again. "Sean, you okay, mate?"

This time, Sean responded, "Yeah, I am." He hesitated, then added, "There was something I wanted to tell you, Conor."

"Okay. What is it?"

"Well, it's that … no, not tonight. Maybe another time."

He was not making sense.

"Are you sure you're okay?" Conor asked again.

"I'm just not myself at the moment."

"I haven't seen you at the Abbey View this week, mate."

"No, no … not been."

"Cause you're not feeling yourself?" Conor persevered.

"No, not been great."

"Sorry to hear that. You had a bug or something?" asked Conor.

"Not really, but I've been down, you know, out of sorts. I get like this now and then. Nothing for you to worry about."

"Well, we've missed you," added Conor. "And what you are doing out so late, mate? It's snowing, and you've no coat."

"Aw, well, yes, I was in a rush you see. I was feeling anxious, a bit claustrophobic at home in my little one-bed flat. I just wanted some space and some fresh air. I wasn't really thinking straight, so I didn't pick up my coat. I come here to the abbey because of the space … and this place reminds me of somewhere. A place I used to spend a lot of time when I was younger. Happy memories, you know. Always makes me feel better. Of course, that was a very long time ago."

"Ha, you're not that old, Sean, are you now."

"I'm sixty-one."

"See, I was right, a spring chicken. You're about the same age as my mammy and daddy. I know what you mean about this place; it's funny you should say it reminds you of somewhere. That's why I come here too. The abbey reminds me of home."

"Where is that then, home?" asked Sean.

"Right now, it's James Bridge, Yorkshire, but my childhood home, where my family are, is Dunstan. Do you know it?"

Sean nodded. "Yes, I've heard of it. Your family is still there?" he asked.

"Yes. Mammy, Daddy and Marie, my sister."

"You have a sister?"

"Yeah, a younger sister. She used to be a pain following me around everywhere. I'm eight years older, but we're close."

"I have a younger brother. I know what you mean about younger siblings following you everywhere. Relying on you." Sean was momentarily lost in thought, then added, "I'd better be off home to get warm, then."

"Yes, mate, me too. Look after yourself. Hope to see you at the Abbey View soon. Night, mate," he said.

"Night, mate," replied Sean.

Chapter Three

Conor worked throughout the festive period. He
had had his Christmas dinner alone, reheated
after closing time. He had been working so hard
to try and push past this sadness and stress he
was feeling. This evening, Sean stayed at closing
time and kept Conor company while he cleaned
and cashed up.

"How are things, Sean?" Conor asked.
"Feeling better?"

Sean paused before replying, "Aw, you
know, okay," he answered. I'll be cracking jokes
and be the fun storyteller again any day now. I'll
not be the crazy guy lurking in the shadows at
the abbey at midnight like the headless monks,
with no coat on when it's snowing and scaring
people."

"Can I tell you something?" Conor asked
Sean.

"Yeah, yeah, you can. I'm listening."

"I-I've not been feeling great myself. Last
night, I went to bed. I closed my eyes. My body
was tired, but my mind just wouldn't quiet. It
got louder and louder, like a big movie screen,
playing all my mistakes from years ago. My
inner voice turned into a bully, berating me for
getting older, for not being a better person, for
not being able to think my way out of this

anxiety and find a solution. I couldn't stand it anymore. My body couldn't relax; I couldn't breathe. I felt trapped. I walked out my front door, and before I knew it, I was at the abbey, standing on the cold, wet grass in my bare feet. Embarrassed to walk home in case anyone saw me."

"Oh, my god," said Sean. "Can I help?"

"No, I don't think you can, mate."

Sean downed the last mouthful of his pint. "Well, I'll be here again tomorrow if you want to talk."

It was midnight when Conor locked up. The air was crisp and clear, frost sparkling on the ground. As he walked home past the abbey, he thought about the headless monk and about Sean. How could talking to Sean again help him when he didn't know how to help himself? He thought of the adage "a problem shared is a problem halved", but he wasn't sure this was always the case. Sean was a man of few words, so his advice might be meagre, but at least he would not be subjected to unsolicited advice or worse, be told to get over himself.

His current state of mind was scaring him. He did not feel like himself anymore. It was like something had broken, but he could not find what it was to fix it. He wasn't happy, but he hadn't changed anything in his life and had been content enough with it before. Once home and ready for bed, Conor snuggled up in the warmth of his blanket and tried to relax. *The end of another day*, he thought.

Conor decided he would talk to Sean again. At least he knew he wouldn't judge him after finding him at the abbey. He had found it easy to speak with him tonight. However, he did not find the time to talk to him again.

Then he began to put distance between Sean and himself as he pretended that he was okay, his way of coping with the fact that he was really not okay.

***

As the seasons changed from winter to spring, so too did the atmosphere in James Bridge. The quiet winter months with the odd coach trip arriving now and then were past. The town began to come alive again with the arrival of many more visitors. The spring flowers around the abbey's lake ushered in the new season with vibrant colours: yellow daffodils, crocuses of purple, yellow, lavender, cream and white, and white, orange and yellow primroses. Lambs gambolled in the fields; the alpacas would soon have their young crias, and Conor could watch them playing from his window.

Families arrived at the lake with picnic boxes packed with tasty treats: sandwiches, strawberries, grapes, cakes, mini savoury snacks, crisps and dips. The children enjoyed the dry weather as they could roll down the grassy slopes surrounding the abbey, and dogs playfully joined in too.

Laughter filled the air, and there were so many daisies and buttercups to be picked, the buttercups held under chins with cries of "You like butter!" and "Mummy, Mummy, please let's make a daisy chain." After carefully seeking out the longest, thickest stems, the daisies were threaded together to make necklaces, crowns, and bracelets. The pretty little white flowers, occasionally with a pink sweep of colour underneath, closed at night and then opened to enjoy the sun, just like an eye, "day's eye", opening, the centre like an eyeball and the tiny petals the eyelashes. The days were longer now, and James Bridge was alive, the abbey no longer lost in darkness but hailing its magnificence as it stood tall and proud in the spotlight of the sun, reaching skyward like the spring flowers as if new life had been breathed into it, no longer enclosed but now with the beautiful skies as a ceiling. White fluffy clouds of different shapes and sizes billowed across the bright blue sky — nature, the most beautiful artist. Spring, the time when, for the Cistercian monks, abundance returned to the land they tended around the abbey and the better days returned.

But something that had not sprung into life was Conor. He had distanced himself from everyone, including Sean. In denying that anything was wrong, he had thrown himself into work, too busy to socialise or to play music. The unspoken pretence of everything being "okay" and the continuing charade between himself and the rest of the world was his coping strategy. It was as though he was lost in winter still, even though the season had passed. But Conor had stayed in the darkness. He did not want to stay there in the shadow of winter.

Conor wanted to help Sean, but how could he even begin to help unpack his problems when he had so many of his own? Conor's unhappiness had not happened overnight. It was not a sudden disaster or a major life event that had left him feeling so mentally exhausted. It had been a gradual creeping in of stress over time that had led him to this unhappy place. And every day, as he carried on with a life that no longer worked for him, he became more unhappy and unfulfilled. And as it was his own life, he could not look at the situation objectively to figure it out.

Every day, Conor was trudging on in the same way, in the same life, with the same routines because once they had made him happy. He couldn't understand that he had changed; therefore, his needs had changed.

Sean also wanted to help Conor. He could see he had changed. Sean had the experience of living different lives and evolving, but he had reached the point where he did not know how to talk to Conor about this. It was difficult because it reminded him of the traumatic events of his own life. Hopefully, as they headed further into spring, a time of new beginnings, things would start to look up.

***

Conor opened his front door, stepped outside and held his face upward towards the sun, closing his eyes and basking in its glory. Reawakening his senses and remembering how the sun felt after a long winter. Today was going to be a busy day. Ten coach trips were already booked in for lunchtime. He was not looking forward to welcoming them all, but at least being so occupied was the distraction he needed.

Keep going, keep busy, work hard. This was his life.

He felt alone. He had done a great job isolating himself from his family, easy to do as the sea divided them. It had been twenty years since he left for England, now his home. He had left full of enthusiasm for the future. *Yes, Mammy, I'm fine* he would say on the phone. *Yes, yes, still enjoying work. So, what have you been up to?* He would bat the questions back to his mammy, who was happy to talk for hours. What would she say to him if she knew he was no longer happy with the life he had chosen? If she knew she had sacrificed years of seeing her son in person for a life that did not fill him with joy. He had not become a successful musician. He had not travelled the world. He was single, still, and lonely. He had no children. He missed home but could not return as this failed version of himself.

Isolating himself from his co-workers had been harder. But he had decided he would rather they thought him rude than them thinking he was going crazy. Conor himself thought he was going crazy, but others thinking that was not okay.

All his youthful enthusiasm had not just dwindled; it had rotted and become something else, something dark and twisted. He thought of that version of himself and desperately despised it. He was still young, thirty-eight, but he did not feel it. He felt old as the stress he was carrying seeped out of his body in ways he could no longer control. With his quick humour and Irish accent, now with the tiniest sprinkle of the local Yorkshire twang, he had once been the most entertaining barkeeper in James Bridge. He didn't miss a beat. He made everyone feel welcome, and they all loved him. The visitors and the locals were thrilled when he brought his bodhrán drum for a singalong. The guests at the Abbey View even loved his home town favourite, "Lovely Laois", and would request it and sing along.

Lovely Laois. I hear you calling in my dreams; I hear you say, come back home to dear old Ireland.
Lovely Laois, I'll come back to you one day.

With a voice like silk, he did not miss a note. But he had not picked up the bodhrán for months. It sat in a corner gathering dust, another reminder of the person he had somehow lost. The one thing that always brought him joy was now not part of his life. It only reminded him of how unhappy he was and how he did not know how to change that.

Conor was still having nightly panic attacks. He coped well during the day, busy with work, but at night, as the room fell silent and he tried to close his eyes, his mind became loud — thoughts jumping in one after the other, like an overloaded conveyor belt. Sean, the one person in whom he had confided, he had pushed away. There was now a distance between them. Conor did not blame him as he would distance from himself if he could. Now, the only company he had was his own, and lately, that was not pleasant.

***

Conor was busy serving the customers, standing three rows deep at the bar. It was so busy he didn't have time to think. *Yes, how are you today? What can I get you?* He made eye contact with the customers and smiled while working as quickly as possible to get the queue moving. There was a jolly atmosphere among the visitors, who had been enjoying their visit to the town. It was soon time to close. He had taken to working double shifts over the winter and had not yet changed his name on the rota. With the stints getting busier, he was starting to feel tired from work and lack of sleep. He made a mental note to take this on board when he did next month's rotas. He had more casual staff joining over the spring and summer months.

As he put up the last bar stool, he paused and thought of Sean. This evening's visitors would have loved his tales. But he only allowed himself that one moment of reflection and then shooed it from his head. He shut the door to the Abbey View and secured it behind him. *Another day done,* he said to himself. *Another day done,* he repeated, then wandered home to bed.

The blossom on the trees showered the children playing in its shade like confetti. They giggled and screeched in excitement. A cool breeze was blowing, but it was another beautiful sunny spring day with the promise of summer and brighter things to come. Long days and good times.

Conor wished he had time to stop and join in with the fun. It was his day off, but he had chores to do and groceries to replenish; although he mostly ate at work, he still needed milk, coffee, cereal, washing powder, loo roll, handwash, bread, jam and cheese. All these daily items were on his list, plus a bar or two of chocolate and a bottle of wine.

He had to go to the post office with his sister's birthday present—his little sister Marie, thirty next week—then to the cobbler's to pick up the shoes he had taken to be reheeled. No point throwing them out if they can be repaired, he had thought. As he passed the ice cream parlour, families with young children held up the queue as they could not decide between strawberry or chocolate ice cream. Conor laughed to himself. He quite fancied an ice cream. He would choose cinder toffee flavour with a flake and extra toffee sauce squirted on top. His sister would have strawberry all day long, and strawberry sauce. She would give the flake a miss and opt for rainbow sprinkles. Thinking of Marie and the ice cream made him smile, but the queue was too long, and he did not have time to stop and treat himself.

He returned home, carrying his bags of shopping. He had popped in a bottle of wine or two, which made the load heavier. He unpacked, satisfied that everything was in its place, then removed the four scratch cards he had purchased at the checkout from his jeans pocket. He found a coin and scratched away. Not this time, he thought. He went to the cupboard, poured a glass of red wine, and popped his meal-for-one beef lasagne into the microwave. *Ping!* He carefully carried the hot plate to the table using a tea towel. He placed it on a mat and finally sat down. Sinking into the chair, he took a deep breath and said aloud, even though no one else was there to hear, "Another day done."

Chapter Four

It was 4 am. Conor had maybe had a few hours of fitful sleep. He was conscious of being awake but was completely paralysed as he lay on his back staring at the ceiling. Shadows in his room crept towards him as he tried to call out but only made a muffled sound. A figure loomed over him. Why couldn't he move? What did the figure want? He could not even call for help, not that anyone would hear him. He was frightened. Frightened and alone. Helpless. He woke again at 6 am; he must have fallen back asleep. This time, he could move and was fully awake and mobile. *Jesus Christ*, he thought, *what the hell happened?*

What a horrendous experience. Was it real? Was it a dream? It felt real. A deep sadness settled within him, and he started to cry. He sat on the floor, hugging his knees, releasing his sadness. He was tired, so tired. He didn't want to go back to bed as the experience had frightened him, but he didn't have a choice; his sleep-deprived body wanted to. So, he climbed back into bed and stayed there all day, finally sleeping eight hours, waking again at 3 pm. He felt a release. A good cry and a full sleep.

Conor knew he needed to take better care of himself and address what was happening, but he was not sure he had the energy. He'd turned himself into some sort of villain. He was so convinced he was stuck here in this place, in this state of eternal damnation. He would tell himself he deserved it. He should have done more with his life. He had not been home for a while as he did not want the eyes of disappointment cast upon him. *You are totally useless*, his inner voice said to him. He used to have a kinder inner voice that would interject and keep him more balanced. It would say things like *you work hard, and you're tired, but everything will be okay. You are kind and enjoy life, especially music and entertaining with your drum. You're strong and capable.* But he had even succeeded in pushing away that kind inner voice, or it had abandoned him, driven away with all the negative thinking, tension and stress that caused his fight or flight system to kick in every evening. It was black down here in this hole, and very lonely.

***

Conor was busy serving a large group of visitors who had just arrived at James Bridge after a long journey. Orders were flying in thick and fast: breakfast buns and cups of tea, full English breakfast and fresh orange juice. He had just taken an order for a vegan breakfast with a coffee, and as he looked up from the bar to smile at the customer, he saw Sean.

He was busy, swamped, no time to say hello. Sean was not important right now; the customers were and needed his full attention and best service. He noticed Sean take his usual seat just at the edge of the bar as another staff member took his order. Conor noted that he'd asked for a full English with black pudding. He smiled as he thought of Sean joking and complaining about the lack of white pudding. *You will have to get your Mammy to send some over.* Conor smiled to himself at the memory but again shooed it away and returned his attention to the breakfast orders. He had to focus on work, not on Sean. But later, as he watched Sean leave, he could not shake the thought of him.

He was still thinking about him as he walked home. Sean used to be his friend. They used to look out for each other. What had happened? Maybe he should reach out to him, but he was busy. Very busy with work.

***

While they represent destruction and decay, there is an undeniable beauty in ruined buildings. They stand as a link to now and another time. As you wander around them, the unenclosed atmosphere saturates the ground and streams into the sky. The time of year you visit, the weather at the time, and the light all evoke feelings in the setting, calling on distant tales of the past.

The ruined abbey sits wistfully by the water's edge, casting stunning reflections into the lake. The reflections are almost as real as the two versions of the abbey meet together in harmony, only the occasional ripple in the water distorting the image. The abbey stands proud; it has accepted its ruinous status, making it more magnificent. It has survived and it is celebrated. A landmark people would purposefully make their destination.

You could sometimes see visitors standing in the centre of the ruins, eyes tight shut as if closing their vision made their other senses more powerful — to hear the buildings, to connect to those that once lived there. Creating images in their mind's eye of what it may have been like long ago.

The monks would visit the infirmary at least four times a year for bloodletting as they believed it rebalanced the body and soul and gave you a more beautiful voice. Conor used to think this was madness, but now, feeling ever more connected to this place, he would quite happily have given the bloodletting a chance — anything to change his current situation.

Conor sat late one evening in the abbey cloister, where the monks used to spend time in meditation and prayer. Monks had to adhere to complete silence in this area and would use sign language to communicate. This is also where the abbot would wash the monks' feet in the way Jesus washed the disciples' feet. He pondered why he always came to the abbey for comfort and when he was feeling anxious. Perhaps it was the spiritual connection with the Catholic monks or that, despite the abbey's ruinous state, all he could see was beauty. Something calmed him here.

He decided to take the audio tour of the abbey, though he had taken it many times before and knew it word for word:

And here we have the warming house. This is where a fire would burn from November to Easter. Every monk was allowed just fifteen minutes a day by the fire. Next, we come to the library. Monks would read and meditate here. The library was small as it would take one monk three years to write one copy of the bible.

He thought about the monks living here. Were they content with their life of service? Did they ever utter words instead of using sign language when it was time to be silent?

Conor believed the stories and the decay of the building made it more of a landmark, more awe-inspiring. Perfect was not interesting. Life was interesting. The abbey's marks and scars were part of the majesty of the place. Weirdly, the narration on the audio headphones calmed him. They took him out of his head and into the past.

He suddenly noticed a sign that said Private, Personnel Only. How had he never come across that before? He moved closer, running his hand over the lock on the thick wooden door reinforced in iron. It dawned on him that this was a keyhole for a four-pronged key. His key would fit!

He felt in his coat pocket and pulled out the key Bobby had made him. He had all but forgotten it was there. It had been sitting in this jacket pocket since Christmas. Curiosity got the better of him, and he lifted the key to the lock, and to his amazement, the key easily slipped into the lock. He looked around to see if anyone was watching. It was late, and no one else was around. *Bobby, what game are you up to?* This must be some elaborate joke. He pushed the key fully into the lock and gave it a twist to see if it would turn. It did not. He gave it another wiggle. Nothing. Suddenly, he heard footsteps behind him and turned quickly to see who was there. No one. He took the key out of the lock and put it back into his pocket. He placed his hand in his pocket and rubbed his thumb and forefinger over the key. He found it comforting, like a fidget toy for kids. He headed home, wondering how on earth Bobby knew about the keyhole.

Chapter Five

Sean was on his way to Bobby's workshop. He often popped in to watch Bobby work. They would then have a cuppa and a chat. Sean walked into the workshop expecting to see Bobby mid-presentation of his ironmongery skills, making nails for tourists. He was surprised to find nobody there and the workshop closed.

Sean went through the overgrown side garden and stood on a brick in the soil to look through the workshop window. Nothing. Not even an ember on the coal pile. *Very strange*, he thought. He was also disappointed, as he was hoping Bobby would teach him a few more ironmongery skills. Sean had been learning to make nails.

Curiosity driving him, he ventured further round to the bungalow at the back of the workshop. He could see Bobby through the open kitchen window and was about to call out his name when he realised someone else, obscured from view, was there, and it looked like they were engaged in a tense conversation. He sensed he should not interrupt, so he left and returned home.

Conor and Bobby were deep in conversation in Bobby's kitchen. Two half drunken cups of cold tea sat on the table. "And you started making keys like the one you gave me for Christmas after the archaeology dig they undertook at the abbey twenty years ago?"

"Yes," said Bobby. "As you know, I have a knack for making key decorations."

"Yeah, like the Santa keys you made for the Christmas tree at Abbey View."

Bobby nodded and went on to explain that keys became important to the monks when the Vikings invaded as they realised that monasteries had treasures to steal. Before this, the monks did not need locks and keys. No one would have stolen from God. But the Vikings were not Catholic, so they had no care for the religious consequences; they just cared for the wealth.

Monasteries were easy targets for the Vikings as they were isolated, did not house soldiers, and were full of valuable commodities of silver, gold and other precious materials. It made sense to the monks to make the abbey more secure and have thick wooden doors covered in metal and locked with iron keys.

"So," continued Bobby, "I started making keys for the tourists to buy from my workshop. Did you know your key would fit the lock at the abbey?"

"No," said Bobby with a grin, completely intrigued that his keys might open something, though a tad unsure of the legal implications of making copies of keys that actually opened something.

"Have you any more keys like this one?" asked Conor, who now also wore a huge grin.

"I'll fetch them," Bobby said.

He left the kitchen for a moment and returned with a shoe box. He opened the lid and emptied the contents onto the table.

Not quite believing he was planning on finding the key to open a door that did not belong to him and might get him into trouble, Conor surprised himself by revealing it needed to have four prongs to fit the lock, a bit different a design to the one he now produced from his jacket pocket. Bobby nodded, thought and looked. He pointed out a key to Conor.

"Now, yes, this one." He held up a key and added, "Do you know Lisa who works at the abbey?"

"Yes, she comes into the Abbey View for lunch sometimes."

"Yes, she was having lunch there when I saw a set of keys on her belt, and we got talking about my keys and the monks and the Vikings. I had a bacon sandwich — white bread, brown sauce."

"Yes, yes," said Conor impatiently, "I know what you had, Bobby; it's what you always have! What's that got to do with this key?"

"She had one key in her collection that caught my eye. Chunky—four prongs, a ball of iron on the end. She said it didn't open anything, that it had just been passed to her with the keys to the museum when she got the job nearly twenty years ago, and she just presumed it was a keyring. I asked if I could take an impression of it to make a copy for my collection. And since it didn't open anything, she was happy to oblige I made two different copies."

"And these are the keys?"

"Yes, and look, very similar to yours, aren't they?"

Conor's eyes widened, holding the keys side by side. "Yes, they are."

"You have them," Bobby said to Conor, "and you will tell me if it works, and you can open the door? You'll let me know?"

"Of course," said Conor. He turned to leave but then looked back. "Oh, I forgot to ask. What are the symbols on the keys?"

"Ah, yes, a good question. The monks employed masons to build the abbey, paid by the number of stones finished. To ensure they received the correct payment, each Master Mason signed his stones with an original mark, known as 'mason's marks', made of shapes and lines. So, I thought it would be a nice touch to add some of the Master Mason's marks to my keys."

"Fascinating, Bobby. I'll see you soon," said Conor, winking at Bobby as he left.

"See you soon," Bobby replied.

***

That evening, straight after work, Conor made his way to the abbey. Although the abbey was always accessible, he knew the guided tours and the museum would be closed, and he had never seen anyone else there at close to midnight.

He approached the library, glanced round his shoulder, and took the narrow, arched passage to the door he had found. He took the two new keys out of his pocket and switched on the torch light on his phone, holding it in one hand while he examined the keys in the other. Both Master Mason's symbols differed from the first key Bobby had given him as a gift at Christmas. One key had an equilateral triangle with two parallel lines running through it from top to bottom, and the other had a star shape,

resembling the asterisk key on a keyboard.
Conor examined the lock more closely
this time, shining his torch light directly onto it.
He decided to use the equilateral triangle key
first. He carefully but nervously, fearing getting
caught, put the key into the lock. It did not go all
the way in. He tried again to make sure. *Nope,
not that one.* He carefully put that key back in his
pocket to avoid losing it. He tried the next key.
In it went. A perfect fit. He turned the key, and
clunk. The tips of his fingers tingled with
excitement and trepidation. He gave the door a
forceful push, and it opened.

Conor was half expecting alarm sirens
signalling his entrance into the restricted
personnel area. Nothing. No sound, but then, no
one would have expected someone to have a
copy of such an old key, would they, he
reassured himself.

It was dark, too dark to see the whole
room, so Conor inspected the area piece by
piece, using the light on his phone. *I should have
brought a proper, more powerful torch*, he scolded
himself. As he stepped inside, the door creaked
and closed behind him. He stopped in his tracks,
but there was no way he was turning back now.
He first inspected the room at eye level —
standing on the spot and turning in a circle to
determine how big the room was. It was small;
he estimated it to be about one-metre square.

Stone walls. He looked up to the ceiling. More stone arching. It was not far above his head. He estimated it to be roughly two metres at the highest point.

He focussed the torch from the base of the wall up to where it met the ceiling, section by section. He did not know what he was looking for, but he was determined to search until he found it. He couldn't see anything, just bare stone walls. It appeared to be an empty room. But Conor sensed it was not. He knew there was a reason he had found that key.

He shone the phone torch down towards his feet. And that's when he saw the most beautifully preserved ceramic floor tiles, locking together to make geometric shapes. He probably should not be walking on them, he thought. He took a step back to admire the colours of yellow and red. As he moved, he stood on a couple of loose tiles and remained still before taking some small, considered steps backwards as if walking a tightrope. Suddenly, he heard a voice outside. He did not want to get caught breaking and entering, so he decided, when all was quiet, he would lock up and come back tomorrow with a better torch.

***

Conor's dream was so unpleasant that it meant anxiety had even followed him into his time of rest: He sits at a small hexagon-shaped table in the corner of a large, empty room painted white. His sister is beside him at the table, strapped into their chairs like a fairground ride about to take off. They sit facing the far wall, which is completely solid—no windows, no doors, just white. Behind them is a door to the outside and a small window. Conor can only half turn his head to look behind and out of the open door as he is strapped tight.

A young woman enters the room. "Hello," his sister addresses the woman, who stops, startled.

"Who said that?" She scans the room, looking through them as if she cannot see them.

"Hello," says Conor. This time, she screams and runs out the open door. Conor looks at Marie, confused. A look she returns. Conor turns his head, straining his neck to look out of the open door. Everything outside has grown; the small shoots of grass now tower over the house. Suddenly, a giant's hand, holding a dustpan and brush, begins sweeping up the soil outside. The room shudders slightly. It feels like they are doll-sized in a little dolls house that now feels flimsy and unstable. Is this why they are strapped in? As quickly as it had started, the shaking stops. Three people enter the room.

Two men and a woman. Conor deduces they are in their sixties. They are well dressed, in tailored black trouser suits. The men wear gold watches, and the woman has a string of pearls around her neck. One of the men is carrying a book under his arm, holding it very tightly. They move towards Conor and Marie. They take Conor's cap from his head. He can't take it back because he is strapped to the chair, so they make fun of him. They take Marie's Claddagh ring from her finger. Conor feels enraged and shouts out for them to stop. The man carrying the book takes something from his pocket. He holds it up against the white wall. It is a large iron key. He throws it at Conor, and it spins in slow motion across the room through the air and hits Conor directly in the mouth. He abruptly wakes, disoriented and nauseous, his heart pounding in his chest. He is lying face down on the cold ground. He pushes himself to a sitting position and spits grass out of his mouth. He puts the back of his right hand to his mouth. Blood. His top lip is split and bleeding. He looks around. He is in the abbey cloister. *What on earth am I doing here*, he thinks, his heart racing, head thumping. He had been sleepwalking. His night terrors, stress and anxiety had reached a whole new depth. He felt shaken. He knew he had to address what was going on, where the pressure in his life could be lessened. Where the loneliness and isolation could be broken. He walked home, bewildered.   As he approached, he saw that his front door was wide open. He must have left it like that. He was thankful not to have been burgled or visited by some stray animal.

***

All the staff and customers have left Abbey View. Conor has completed all his jobs, and he is ready for "Mission Abbey Secret Room". He has his powerful torch, which he had remembered to fully charge when he got home last night. And he has "the key". He had thought the day would never end. It inched along so slowly, but now it was time. He could not walk quickly enough,
but he wanted to look casual in case anyone might spot him. He could see the abbey up ahead. He was so excited. The most excited he had been about anything for a while.
As he got closer, he scouted for signs that no one else was around. His eyes scanned the grounds, and he made his way to the library, his ears on high alert for any sound. As he entered the low archway, he readied his torch and his key. He felt like a monk hiding treasure from

58

invading Vikings. He was really enjoying himself.

He unlocked the door and gently stepped inside, avoiding the loose tiles. The torch he had brought this evening was bigger and brighter. He could see so much more in one beam. He shone it down, scouring the floor and stopping at the tiles he had unsettled the night before. He thought he had found something. He put the torch down on the floor and got onto his hands and knees, moving the four rickety tiles very carefully so as not to break them. He picked up the torch again, concentrating the beam onto the newly uncovered ground.

Moving those tiles had revealed a hollow space underneath the floor. He could see a piece of parchment. He put his hand into the hole. He could feel something. He desperately hoped he could retrieve it without damaging the surrounding tiles. Conor very slowly lifted the object towards the opening. It reminded him of playing the game Operation as a child.

He could only fit one hand in the hole, steadying himself with the other. Slowly, ever so slowly. *Carefully now, keep going.* Then the paper came into view at the hole, and he could use his other hand to guide it out. As he excitedly lifted his hand, a scroll with a blue ribbon tied around it appeared. He prayed he would not get caught now; he was too far invested in the mystery. So, he would not unwrap it here.

He carefully replaced the loose tiles over the hole, gently stepped backwards to the door and exited. He took the key from his pocket and locked the door. He peered out of the low archway to check the coast was clear. No one. He placed the mysterious, wrapped object under his jacket and walked home.

Once back at his flat and safely out of view, Conor removed the scroll from his coat and carefully placed it on the table. He felt both desperate and anxious; he likened the feeling to receiving his university degree results. He gently removed the ribbon and unrolled the scroll with the intricately written title, "Enlightenment of the Soul" — breathtakingly beautiful. He wondered who had placed it there. It read:

> *The night of the dark soul, the lost.*
> *Searching the mind at all cost,*
> *Searching the body for an issue, what's gone*
> *wrong, what isn't working right?*
> *Trying to bring it out into the light.*
> *Ignored for so long.*
> *Days spent with affirmations and gratitude.*
> *Don't look at the dark or the shadows, stay*
> *strong.*
> *But this is wrong.*

*Ignoring it makes it grow. It wants to be
known. It needs to be seen.
Or it will take control of your body, even in
your dreams.
I do not disguise this feeling when I am
grateful.
I don't want to see blackness, a world that is
so hateful.
Dear soul, please Enlighten my body.
Let my body follow your lead.
Dear soul, please tell me what you need.
This is the night of the dark soul.
So lost and so alone.
I cannot find my way out of the darkness. The
more I ignore it within myself, the more it
takes hold.
I must change this trajectory.
I must do something bold.
I must face the dark to find the message of my
soul.*

The mystery of the origins of the scroll
had spun Conor's head that night, making it
difficult for him to get to sleep. Something about
the words seemed so familiar. Had he seen the
poem written somewhere before? The words
made him feel uncomfortable inside. It was as if
he was transported to a particular, unpleasant
feeling that he could not put a name to.

He was tired this morning. Luckily, it was his day off. He had planned to update Bobby today, so, once he was up and dressed, he headed off to Bobby's blacksmith shop.

As he walked up the drive, he could hear the clanging of metal against metal, and he could feel the heat from the coal. Bobby nodded to acknowledge his arrival. Conor watched him work, mesmerised by the orange sparks each time Bobby hit the metal. On completion, Bobby used tongs to dip his masterpiece in the water. It hissed and steam rose. He removed a glove and tapped his fingers on the metal to test the temperature. When he was sure it was cool enough to be handled, he passed it over to Conor. It was a large, square-headed nail with two initials on the top — JR. It was for one of the tourists, who would be collecting it later. He had already made eight that morning and had eight more to go. Conor admired Bobby's handiwork. "Something small the visitors to James Bridge can take home with them," said Bobby. "Personalised," he added. "Something I can make a few of in a day."

Conor nodded. "Nice," he said running his fingers across the initials.

"Anyway," said Bobby, "you've not come to talk about nails, have you?"

Conor smiled. "No, I've not. Well said,

Bobby."

"Did the key work?" asked Bobby. "Yes, yes it did."

"And?" Bobby was growing impatient.

"And … I found a very small room, more like a cupboard, to be honest. Bobby listened intently. "I think the reason the door has been placed there is to preserve the original flooring. It is quite spectacular. A few tiles are a bit loose, and underneath the loose tiles was a secret hole." He had Bobby's full attention. "I found something there."

"In the hole?" asked Bobby.

"Yes, in the hole. It was a scroll with a poem on it called the 'Enlightenment of the Soul'. It has been hand written in calligraphy, but it's not old. It's new. Someone else knows about the room. Someone put it there recently, and I'm going to find out who."

"I would ask Lisa," said Bobby, "but I don't want her to know that you are breaking into the abbey and that I gave you the key."

"Yes, best not ask her. Could it be her's, even? But then why would she have let me copy the key if she wanted to hide something?"

"Good point, Bobby."

Conor woke in his bed. He could feel a breeze on his arms from underneath his bedroom door. As he stepped out of bed to investigate, he noticed his feet covered in dirt. He opened his bedroom door and was shocked to find his front door wide open. He quickly shut it, closing out the breeze and before any passers-by could peek into his home. *What on earth*, he thought, but deep down, he already knew why the door was open, and his feet were filthy. He had been sleepwalking again. He was frightened by the experience now. If he was not consciously aware of his actions at night, he could be going anywhere, doing anything, putting himself in danger. Why was this happening to him? He stood there frozen to the spot; his eyes glazed over. He did not know what to do then, so he did nothing.

Eventually, Conor sat down at the table. He had no answers. He did not know why he was having nightmares or why he was sleepwalking, and, more importantly, he did not know how to stop it. He despaired at his helplessness. All he could do was to carry on with his normal routine. *Get ready for work. Deal with it later*, and his body obliged by getting up from the table and heading into the shower. He just kept going in the direction he knew. The regimen he knew like the back of his hand, simply because he did not know what else to do.

It was approaching midnight, and Conor was back at the abbey. He did not go straight to the secret room. He sat on the grass bank, where he had a direct view of the arched entrance to the mysterious room. He had been sitting there for about half an hour, watching and waiting, wondering if he would see anybody enter. He decided he had had enough of waiting and stood up to go. He had the key, two torches this time and a bag. He entered the room carefully as, despite his intrigue, he did not want to damage the ancient floor.

He placed one torch down on the ground and held the other. First, he checked under the loose tiles, picking them up with great care. Nothing. He then began scanning with the torch, section by section, floor to ceiling, ceiling to floor. He started at the door and meticulously worked his way round. When he got to the second corner, ceiling to floor, he thought he saw something. His heart raced. He moved to that corner of the room and shone the torch directly onto the floor. *What the heck is this?* Writing. There was writing—in red chalk. "**Me**" was the first word he saw. He stepped back to illuminate the whole floor. It read: "**Please help me**." He loosened his grip on the torch as he suddenly got chills. It was not excitement he was feeling anymore; it was fear.

He held the torch tighter and checked the words again. "**Please help me.**" Was the message for him? Had somebody seen him here? If so, who was it? What sort of help did they need? Perhaps it was a trick! Did Bobby have another key? Did he think it would be funny? It did not feel funny. Conor had a knot in his stomach. He had desperately hoped to find something, but now he was not sure.

He sat down in the opposite corner of the room, keeping his torch and his eyes focused on the writing as if it were some wild animal that would pounce and devour him if he broke eye contact. He felt startled, scared even. He studied the words. Three simple words. Why were they so chilling? Eventually, he got to his feet after the adrenaline had subsided and his heartbeat returned to normal. But he left feeling someone was watching him.

***

Conor was so tired. He was living on a minimal amount of sleep and energy. He crawled through to the end of each day, and there was little release when he got home from work.

This evening, as every evening, his coat lay on the doormat, and his shoes had been kicked off and left wherever they had landed. He had just enough energy to sink into the armchair nearest the door. Then, he just sat there, staring out the window into the darkness. He was too tired to think. He was not living anymore, merely surviving. Maybe if he had enough energy to think, he could take some kind of action to make the smallest improvements to help his mental health.

An hour passed; he knew he should wash his face, brush his teeth, put on clean pyjamas. He knew it, but he could not do it. It felt like the most enormous and impossible task to complete. He had functioned all day, and now his body and mind were saying no. He eventually fell asleep there in the armchair, fully dressed in his work clothes.

His unconscious mind dived in and out of vivid scenes. People he knew, people he didn't know, and some starting out as one person and then turning into another. What did the unconscious mind know? What did it want to tell him? Waves of water rushed towards him as he tried to reach higher land. He saw tiny chocolate box houses with white wooden shutters behind a gate that towered above and seemed to touch the sky. A man was holding the gate open for him, smiling and beckoning him to come. The water was up to his waist now, and people were sailing past him in rowing boats and canoes. He desperately tried to reach the gate as the man tapped his watch. The opposite gate closed firmly shut, sealing out the water. Conor was swimming now, and the man started to close his side of the gate. He wanted Conor to make it, but he would not wait any longer. Conor was desperately swimming to the gate, the waves high, but he was so close now. A huge wave crashed over his head. Everything turned black. Did he make it?

He woke with a start, his heart pounding, his head thumping, his neck stiff from falling asleep in the chair. It was already morning — time to get going, kick on survival mode yet again. Conor did not feel like he had slept or rested, but he knew he had, because he could remember the dreams. He dragged himself into the shower and lingered a while with his head under the steaming water, not moving, as if frozen. But then he managed to find it. The thing that kept him in his routine, some deep energy reserve. He did wonder, though, when these reserves might run out and desert him.

***

It had been a week since Conor's last visit to the abbey's secret room. He had been back to see Bobby at the forge to tell him about the message. Bobby was sure it must be some practical joke, but Conor was still shaken by the experience. He had thought twice about returning in the dark late at night alone, but his intrigue now overshadowed this feeling.

As he wiped down the bar top at Abbey View, Conor had almost talked himself into going this evening after work. His mind would not let him be free of the thought that he must return. Who else knew about the room? Who had a key? Bobby had sworn he did not have another key, and would he be bothered to play such an elaborate joke on his friend, anyway? Conor didn't think so. *Yes, that was it!* He had decided. He would go this evening as soon as he'd finished tidying down the bar. He could leave the assistant manager to lock up and go before he talked himself out of it.

"You okay to lock up?" he called over to Josey. She nodded, giving Conor a thumbs up.

"No problem," she said.

Conor did a funny half-walk, half-run to the abbey. Now that he had decided to return, he was anxious to get there. What had he missed in a week? Would there be another message waiting for him? What if he caught the other person there; what would he do? He held the key in his pocket. He did his usual 360-degree check before moving in closer. He ducked under the low stone arch and stood straight at the other side. He put his hands on the thick wooden door with impressive metal hinges and lined with a mural. Conor wondered about putting his ear to the door to hear if anyone was inside the room. Then, he thought better of it and decided the door was too solid and thick to hear through. He took his torch out. Then, the key. Every time he looked at it, the more magnificent it seemed to him — the craftsmanship in the shaping of the metal and the weight of it in his hand. He put the key in the lock and took a moment to admire the detail there too: a black metal plate, the left, bottom and right sides all rectangular, but the top an ornate upward curve. Three screws were holding it in place. In the centre was the large keyhole.

Conor thought about peering through the hole but decided that would be pointless due to the blackness within. He placed the key in the lock and enjoyed the clicking sound as it turned. He pushed open the door.

Before stepping inside, he scanned the room with his torch. Once sure no one was inside, he stepped in and closed the door behind him. The dark was so inky black that the torch could only light a small section at a time. He did his usual scan up and down each portion of the small room. This took a while to do thoroughly. Nothing! He felt let down. After a whole week, how could there be nothing? After being so nervous about going, he now stood there, utterly disappointed. Maybe he had missed something by not coming back. He was now cross with himself, convinced his fear had caused him to miss a vital clue. He would return tomorrow.

***

The door clicked as the key turned. He had returned. He would not hesitate tonight. The fire of his fascination had also returned, no longer fearful. He shone the torch directly on the floor. Then began the up-and-down scanning. Conor took it slowly tonight; he did not want to miss anything. He was determined now to solve the mystery of who had left the message for him. He searched and searched. He would not leave until he had found something, another clue, anything.

As he neared the end of his search, he began to lose hope. Then he remembered the compartment under the floor. It was so obvious. This is where he had found the poem the first time, so why had he not searched here last night? He stepped back very carefully over the loose tiles so that they were positioned directly in front of him. He put his torch down gently, carefully removed the tiles, and shone the torch into the small space under the floor. Straight away, the torch reflected off a shiny object. He put his hand into the hole to retrieve it. He stood up, placed the object on his left palm and, using his right hand, shone the torch onto it. A horseshoe. It just filled the palm of his hand and was made from iron. He turned it over to inspect the other side. There was a small impression in the iron at the bend. It was a shamrock. It was a *lucky* horseshoe. Had someone left it there to bring him luck? Or was the one who had left it there in need of a lucky charm and good fortune?

The horseshoe: a universally-known symbol of protection and good luck. The combination of luck, protection and religion has made the horseshoe a good luck charm that wards off evil and misfortune. With its origins in Ancient Greece and Christianity, it was believed that iron could cast off evil, and the crescent shape of the horseshoe symbolised good luck—the iron horseshoe features in the history of most Western nations and India. Horseshoes are traditionally hung with seven nails, as seven is said to be a lucky number. There is also an Irish legend about Saint Dunstan, a blacksmith who nailed a searing hot horseshoe to one of the devil's hooves. This scared the devil, and he would never enter a home with a horseshoe hung above the door.

The shamrock, by definition, is a young sprig of clover. However, botanists say that shamrocks are a distinct species of the clover plant, believed to be the white clover. The word "shamrock" is derived from the Irish "seamróg", which translates as "young clover". Over the centuries, this diminutive plant has come to symbolize Ireland and all things Irish. The shamrock is also a famous symbol of St Patrick's Day. The number three was believed to have magical properties and was a recurring theme in Celtic folklore. Because the Celts were familiar with the shamrock, it became easy to convert their knowledge to the magic of the Holy Trinity. The three leaves are also said to stand for faith, hope and love.

Did the person who wrote the poem and left Conor the message **Please Help Me** need a lucky charm? Did they need faith, hope and love? What help did they need? How could he find them, and would he be able to help them even if he could? Why was this person leaving these items here? Did they know Conor had a key, or had they placed them here for safekeeping, unaware Conor had one? Maybe he should not have removed the poem. Maybe he should not remove the lucky charm if the person needs it. Then, Conor came up with a plan. He could leave a message here in the secret room. The only problem was he had nothing to write with. He decided to go home, write it and then bring it back. It wouldn't take him long. He placed the horseshoe back into the hole and covered it with the tiles. If someone needed a lucky charm, he would certainly not be the one to take it away. He pondered if he should get one for himself.

As Conor walked through the dimly lit streets, he considered what to write on the note. As soon as he was home, he took pen to paper. After a few drafts his final note read:

> *I have a key to this room. If you need help, you can leave a message for me here. I will help you if I can. Can you tell me who you are and what help you need.*
> *From Conor.*

He returned to the abbey to place the note under the floor. Then, all he could do was wait.

Conor returned the following evening, and the note and the horseshoe were still in place, with no sign that anyone had been there. He returned the night after that and the night after that until a week had passed. On the seventh evening, he returned. Conor had quite the routine now. He was an expert at Operation Secret Room: checking for hostiles, having the right torch, moving the tiles. On the seventh evening, the horseshoe and the note were gone. Nothing was in their place. There was no return note, but someone must have been there as they had finally gone after a week of waiting.

Conor returned every night for the next month. Nothing. No clues, messages, poems, lucky charms, or return notes. After that, he stopped going and returned to his routine of focusing on work. Soon, it would be the busiest time of the year for the Abbey View. He needed to hire more casual staff, do the rotas, and up the supply orders. Lots to do. Lots to take his mind off the abbey's secret room and the mysteries it held.

Chapter Six

Spring turned into summer, the peak tourist season. This was the busiest James Bridge got. It was like everything turned up a notch; the people multiplied, the temperature multiplied, and at the Abbey View, the staff multiplied, as did the noise.

Conor was well into his second shift of the day. He had been at work since 8.30 am, and it was now 8.30 pm. It was the height of summer, and, unfortunately, though the bar did have air conditioning, it was not working properly. Conor was convinced it was just blowing hot air around. The customers were queuing five rows deep at the bar. He was sweaty, tired and uncomfortable in his compulsory manager's suit. One of the summer staff members had phoned in sick, so he had not even managed to take his afternoon meal break. He felt woozy, and he had a bad headache as he had not even made time to get a glass of water in the heat. He was too busy keeping the customers happy. He must have been dehydrated as he could not recall going for a wee in the past six hours. Finally, closing time came, and Conor poured himself a pint of water with lots of ice and sat down at the bar. *I did it. Another day done.*

That evening, Conor took his time walking home, enjoying the slight breeze now the sun had set. He was drawn into the abbey and stopped at the lake. Conor took his shoes and socks off and sat down at the water's edge, dipping his feet into the cool water. It felt good, so he leaned forward and splashed his face; it was so refreshing. He looked up towards the sky and then closed his eyes. He was shattered.

He suddenly thought, *Do I need a break from work?* This troubled him as he'd never considered such a thing. *Should I go visit the family? See Marie, make time to have an ice cream with her? Cinder toffee with a flake and toffee sauce?* Conor opened his eyes again and looked down into the still water, where he could see his reflection looking back at him. Conor looked hard at himself as though searching for the answers to the questions he had just asked himself. He looked closely. He didn't just see Conor, the hard worker, the one who'd got it all together; he saw the Conor who lived to work and not the other way round. He could see beyond the Conor who would never admit that his job no longer made him happy.

He put his hand in his pocket and pulled out the contents: the perfectly forged iron key, a torch, a scrap of paper and his lucky charm, an iron horseshoe that could sit in the palm of his hand, with a shamrock on one side. He uncrumpled the note, switched on his torch and read it.

I have a key to this room. If you need Help, you can leave a message for me here. I will help you if I can. Can you tell me who you are and what help you need. From Conor.

For the first time, staring at his own reflection, he did not see the Conor who was determined to persevere, aimlessly hoping it would lead to something, someplace, that would be worth it in the end. He saw Conor, who had not had a holiday from work to visit home in nearly nine years. *Had it really been that long?* He felt shame. He could no longer identify with the Conor, who had convinced him that the feelings of unfulfillment he felt daily would pass. The one who ended each day saying to himself *Another day done*, like if he got enough days done he would finally be rewarded. Just as the Cistercian monks, who lived a simple life of service and solitude, would eventually be rewarded in their afterlife.

Were the monks contented? Did they get rewarded? He looked into the water, and he saw all of himself. Including those parts that he had pushed into the shadows and denied for so long.

He saw the good and the bad, the light and the shade. He saw the truth. The reality. He saw Conor Simon Murphy, born in County Laois, honorary Yorkshireman, who had somehow got split into two denying parts of himself that he had found difficult to deal with, to understand. He sensed his feelings, all of them. He accepted them. Finally, he accepted himself.

Conor had disassociated parts of himself and denied them when they had needed naming and bringing out into the light of day, not hidden in the shadows. He had disowned the part of himself that was no longer happy. This discontent had needed to scream louder and louder to be heard. Instead, it had manifested in the sleepless nights and the anxiety, the lack of joy in the things he used to love as all his energy was spent with his mind signalling his body to cry out for acknowledgement so he could help himself. It had happened so gradually, like the deterioration of the abbey. He had not seen it until he was up to his chin, almost drowning.

Conor had tried so hard to push away every thought and feeling he did not want to experience that he had also smothered all the joy out of his own life. He had done himself a disservice, casting away friends and family with lies that he was okay when he really was not. He did not lie in general, so why had he needed to lie about this? Why had he spent hours making up stories about why he was not as present or why he did not play his bodhrán drum at work anymore? He had said it was getting repaired, and then after a while, he said that the repair shop didn't have the right tools and they needed to order in specialist materials, which may take some time. Then he said he had been so busy that he had not had time to pick it up. Why had he done this to himself? Would the truth not have been easier, have been more freeing than conspiring with the stress and anxiety? Had he fed it? Had he helped it stay hidden in the shadows, helped it grow there as he had felt the shame of it, made it a secret that he was ashamed, embarrassed, scared of?

He looked at the water again. He paused there for a while in reflection. It dawned on him that he was feeling calm, yet his body was still full of tension. He noticed he was holding his breath, so he exhaled, blowing out through his mouth and then big inhales through his nose. He repeated this for a few breaths. He now felt a bit happier, but there was still sadness. Why had he never realised before that opposite emotions could exist together? *What a revelation*, he thought as he moved his gaze from the water up to the abbey. He tried to name what he was feeling. I'm lonely, and I'm homesick, but I feel like I am home here too. I used to love my work but now it makes me unhappy and unfulfilled.

I'm sad that this has happened to me and happy that I am acknowledging all parts of myself. Then he shouted it out loud: "I'M SAD AND I'M
HAPPY!"

Conor hadn't realised that he was not alone. Lisa was working late because of a special event that evening. Although the abbey was free to enter and always open to the public, there were many special events and guided tours that people could pay to participate in—tonight had been one such event: The Abbey Summer LateNight Illuminations. Beautiful colours changed from blue and purple to red, then green, fading in and out, lighting up the whole building.

As well as the light show projecting on the ruins, there was an array of food stalls and a cinema screen showing the history of the abbey. Lisa had been the last to leave, locking up the staff quarters and the small museum next to the abbey, when she saw Conor sitting at the edge of the lake with his feet in the water. She recognised him from the Abbey View. She wondered what he was doing, so she watched him for a moment as he splashed his face with the water from the lake. She walked a bit closer to see if he was okay, thinking it was strange to be sitting there alone at this time of night having a paddle. She heard him shout out I'm happy and I'm sad. She called out to him. "Conor. Conor from Abbey View. Is that you, love? Are you okay?"

Conor was shocked to see someone standing there. He, too, recognised Lisa as a patron at Abbey View. "Hello," he said. Lisa sat beside him on the grass.

"Hi, I'm Lisa."

"Yes, Lisa, I recognised you from Abbey View."

"Yeah, that's right. I love to pop in for a bit of lunch. I like the …", and Conor knew what she was going to say and said it with her… "Jacket Potato, Tuna Salad and Coleslaw."

And Conor added, "… with a cup of milky tea." They both laughed.

"So, love," she said, "are you okay?" The newly awake and aware Conor spoke with honesty. The words just fell out of his mouth before he had even thought about forming them. No need to make up a cover story.

"No, I've not been okay for a while now."

"Sorry to hear that, love. How have you been feeling?" she simply asked.

"Not quite myself," he said. Lisa nodded, encouraging him to continue. "I convinced myself I should be happy because my life had made me happy before, and I ignored the stress and the misery. I thought I had no reason to be unhappy, so I pushed the thoughts further down, making things worse." He paused, but she did not interrupt his thoughts. She just held his gaze, and he continued. "It's only tonight that I've realised that people do change as they get older. What makes them content and happy in life changes too. I've changed." He continued. "It makes sense, doesn't it, that what makes us happy at one point in our lives may, over time, change? I'm not sure why, maybe because I thought I'd be sharing my life with a partner by the time I reached thirty-eight. I'm not, so it makes sense that I need to re-evaluate things?"

"Yes," she said. Conor Simon smiled at her. "And what do you think you do want now?" she asked, then added, "Or don't want anymore?"

Again, she let him think, not interrupting him.

"I want to see my family," he said.

"A good start," said Lisa as she looked into his eyes and waited for more.

"And I want to find a new job, one that suits me as I am now, not when I was in my twenties. I need to take better care of myself. I didn't even stop for a glass of water today."

"But it was twenty-eight degrees," she said to him.

"I know," he said.

"Well, it sounds like you could be taking better care of yourself," Lisa said. He nodded. "But you've some things to start with there, haven't you? What about seeing your family?"

"Yes," he said, "I think you're right. I should go home; it has been such a long time. I seemed to be so busy with work. They are proud of me being a manager, and I wanted to keep doing the thing that made them proud, but by
doing that, I've not been home for years. Crazy, isn't it?"

Then Conor stared at Lisa, right into her eyes, holding her gaze.

"Are you okay, love?" she asked.

"Do you have your keys, Lisa?"

"Yes," she said, more than a little confused. She unhooked the bundle of keys from her belt.

"That one," Conor said.

"This one," she started to say, "it doesn't—" Conor interrupted her, finding his key in the grass with the other items he had emptied from his pocket. He held it up.

"Look," he said. He put the two keys side by side.

"Yes, similar in style," she said. "Nice, aren't they?"

She didn't see, thought Conor. He would not explain to her; he would show her. He got to his feet. "Come with me," he said. For some reason, she trusted him. She switched on her jacket torch and followed him into the darkness. They went through the library. Oh, how she loved the library, her favourite place when she was giving tours around the abbey. For monks, reading was a form of meditation and prayer. She was pulled out of her reverie by Conor directing her to the back of the room and into the far corner arch, which she thought was strange because there was nothing back there; the little stone archway didn't go anywhere. She had always imagined it was where the most precious books were kept, or maybe the books that were being worked on and half-written.

Conor moved out of the main area of the small library, and she followed him. She ducked down beneath the low stone arch. He took a few more steps, as did she, and he shone the torch directly at the lock. He took his key and placed it in the lock. He turned it. Clunk. Then he turned it back. Clunk. He nodded at her, then held up her keys. It was like some elaborate charade he was acting out, and she had to guess. He placed her key in the lock, turning it. Clunk. He smiled and nodded again. He removed the key and handed it back to her. Lisa was bewildered. He pushed the door open. Lisa's jaw dropped. How could this be? How could she not have known this door went somewhere, and how could she have not known that her key opened it? Conor shone his torch inside, Lisa stepped up to the doorway and stuck her head inside. She took her clip-on torch from her jacket to inspect the room further.

Conor pointed the torch beam downwards to illuminate the original tiled floor. Lisa got down on her hands and knees in the doorway, shaking with excitement, to inspect the tiles more closely. Conor moved to step inside the room, but Lisa put her arm out like a barrier to stop him. "No, no!" she said. "Don't walk on it."

"Oh, okay," he said, feeling guilty for all the times he had walked on it, including all the times he was unaware and sleepwalking. Had he been careful in his slumber to remove the tiles, to place the poem and the horseshoe in the space below?

While Lisa was still engrossed in the floor, his mind drifted to thinking about his subconscious. How strange that he thought someone else had had access to the room. Someone else had a key, and it had been himself all along.

The night he realised was about two weeks ago. He had made his way to the abbey while sleepwalking. He had been terrified when he woke up in the darkness. He had panicked at first, frozen to the spot, then as his sense of sight, even with his eyes wide open, was rendered useless, he had used his sense of touch. He put his hands down either side of his body and felt around the floor. He was shaking and tried to take deep breaths to calm himself. It was then he had knocked loose a tile, and it had dawned on him where he was. He had moved his hands up from the floor to his clothes to feel what he was wearing. He had his jacket on. *Inside-right pocket*, he'd thought to himself and searched his person. Yes, relief when he felt his torch. He took it out. Fumbling with the switch, he turned the torch on and shone it down to the floor to confirm his location. He was in the abbey's secret room.

Though relief had started to wash over him, he was still bewildered. He knew he sleepwalked and had terrible night terrors and wild dreams, but he had never come here before. Then he realised he had. He also remembered his mammy sending him the lucky horseshoe with the shamrock about six years ago. He had not needed a good luck charm back then, so he had kept it in the envelope at the back of a drawer in his bedroom.

There had been other bits and pieces in the same drawer, gifts and mementoes. One purchased when visiting an art museum with his then-girlfriend when he was at university. She had thought the poem was intriguing and unusual, and it was cool that it was written on a

scroll. Conor had agreed and bought it to impress her. He had intended to have it framed for his bedroom but never got around to it. Probably because they had split up a month later. It was called "The Dark Night of the Soul".

"How did you know this was here?" Lisa asked him, the question pulling him back to the moment. *Where to start*, he thought, forgetting that when he brought her over here, he had been breaking and entering, or trespassing, or something similar that was not law-abiding.

"Well, it's a long story, but I was given a key as a gift at Christmas, modelled on your key. You remember Bobby asking you, and you said yes, so it wasn't underhand or anything, just a sort of accident. You thought it didn't open anything." Lisa blushed with embarrassment and nodded for him to continue. "And then, between the sleepless nights and the sleepwalking" — she looked confused but did not interrupt — "I was spending a lot of time at the abbey, and the key was in my pocket. Long story short, I found that the key opened the door." He paused and waited for Lisa to scold him. Then she spoke:

"This is amazing. Thank you. Thank you so much." He did not expect that response, so he was a bit speechless. He opened his mouth, but no words came out. She was thrilled, and she was thrilled with Conor.

"No problem," he managed to spurt out.

"Fabulous, isn't it?" she said, looking up at him from the floor, where she was still down on her hands and knees.

"Grand," said Conor.

"And the key itself," she said, "so magnificent, and I've been using it as a keyring." She giggled, seeming happier than ever. "So well-preserved. I'm guessing no one else has been in here since the abbey opened to visitors?"

"No" was the only word that left Conor's mouth.

"What a find. What a find," cried Lisa with joy. "This must be on display, but I don't think we'll want to move it to the museum. Maybe we can make a feature here." Her mind was full of ideas. "I'll have to consult the proper channels in the morning."

Conor nodded in agreement, though he did not know who the "proper channels" were. He started to feel tired. It was really late or really early in the morning, depending on which way you looked at things, and after tonight, he could accept either view. There was no longer a

single angle to view things from in his mind —
the world had somehow shifted.

"Meet me here again tomorrow, in the
daylight. Well, today, I suppose I mean," she
said, looking at her watch. Lisa was still smiling,
but then she looked closely at Conor and said,
"A big night for you, love. Get yourself home to
bed." He nodded and did as he was told.

Chapter Seven

The next morning, Conor did something he had never done before. He made a call and arranged for someone to cover his first shift of the day, and as this meant he did not need to be at work until the afternoon, he went back to bed. He slept until 10 am, showered, and ate a breakfast of pineapple granola with a coffee while watching the alpacas playing from the window. He then made his way to the abbey. He had not agreed on a time with Lisa. It had not crossed his mind to ask last night, and he didn't have her number. He wasn't even sure why she wanted him there. At some point, he would have to warn Bobby that he had told her about the key and the room. He knew Bobby was nervous at his involvement in the "breaking and entering" being uncovered. He must warn him and reassure him it was okay. He would go round to see him at the forge after he had been to the abbey.

When Conor arrived, he headed straight over to the staff building to find Lisa. She was not there. He made his way over to the nolonger-secret door. As he entered the library, he caught sight of her in the stone archway. "Lisa," he called. She popped her head out. She was still grinning.

"Conor," she said, moving towards him. She embraced him like a long-lost family member, which Conor found comforting. It was a nice feeling. "Come see, come see." She was beckoning him to come under the stone arch. The "secret door" was open. There was a cordon up from one side of the door to the other; it resembled a police tape cordon, except it was green and had "of historical importance" written on it. A large floodlight stood at the entrance. With that and it being daytime, it was the best view Conor had had of the room. The reds and yellows of the tiles had transformed in the light and looked more vibrant and more magnificent.

No wonder Lisa had been so excited.

"Look, just look at those geometric shapes and colours."

"Yeah, I can see why you'd be so happy."

"The society are still deciding what to do with them. There's been debate about where a sample should be taken up and placed in the museum, but then, it being such a complete area, it needs to be displayed all together, and why risk breaking them by moving them, so they could be displayed right here with photographs placed in the museum." Lisa glanced at Conor. He looked sad, which made her pause. She had got so swept away with what he had shown her that she had momentarily forgotten why Conor had been at the abbey last night in the first place, how he had been so honest with her, not because they were best of friends, but because she happened to have found him in that moment.

Maybe it was easier to talk to someone who was a passer-by in your life, she thought. Someone who would not break if you told them the truth about your sadness as they were not too invested in you and would soon get swept away by their own life again after that moment. She had proved that to be true, had she not? She had quickly forgotten his problems when the room and the tiles had been revealed to her. She felt bad about this and asked him "How are you?" and paused, keeping eye contact.

"I'm okay," he answered.

"Yeah?" She encouraged him to expand on his answer with her gentle nodding and open body language. Responding, but not talking over him. "It was a busy night, for sure." He halfsmiled. "And did you have time to think about what we discussed, first steps and all that?

Seeing your family?"

"I'm going to ring Mammy later today. Fill her in a bit. See if I can book a flight home for that long overdue visit."

"Well, you get yourself off, love. Do that. I've got this all under control here."

Conor kicked the ground softly a couple of times. "Okay," he said.

"Just one thing," said Lisa. He looked up to face her, wondering what she would say. He met her gaze and paused, waiting. "The key," she said," I'm going to need your key to the door. They one you showed me last night." "Oh. Yes," he said, feeling in his pocket to find it. He had been carrying it around for so long now that it was going to feel strange without it. It had become his good luck charm. It had unlocked more than a door. It had unlocked his subconscious mind and allowed in a part of his himself that had been denied. He had really faced himself. It had taken a while, and he still did not know all the steps he would or could take to help himself, but he was going to try, and if what he tried first failed, he would try again until he got it right. He owed himself this much.   As Conor handed the key over to Lisa, there was a moment where he paused, and they were both holding the key, and he wondered if he would let it go. He did. Lisa thanked him with a smile.

"Good luck, Conor," she said.

"Thanks." He turned to leave the abbey.

Next stop: Bobby's house.

**

"Bobby, Bobby, are you here?" Conor entered the workshop. The coals were still glowing orange, so he wouldn't be far away. "Bobby!" he called again.

"Conor," Bobby said as he appeared from the back door of the workshop. "How are you?"

"Hi," he replied. "I've got an update on the key and the secret room."

"Ah yes, the secret room mysteries that have been keeping us wondering what on earth is going on up at the abbey. What's the latest?"

"Quite a bit, actually—more or less solved, and the secret room is no longer a secret."

"What do you mean no longer a secret?"

"It's okay, not to worry, no one's in any trouble, but Lisa knows what's in it now and that her key opens the door."

"How does she know?"

"I told her." There was a pause as Conor waited for a response, but Bobby didn't have one at that moment in time. So, Conor went on explaining. "You shouldn't worry, though. She knows you didn't know when you made the key. I told her it was me who opened the room. She's just thrilled about the flooring."

"Right," Bobby finally spoke. "Okay." His shoulders dropped. He relaxed again. And what about the poem and the message? What about the lucky horseshoe?"

"Maybe you should make a cuppa, and I'll explain it all to you."

"Yeah, we'll have a brew. I was due a break anyway. I've already boiled the kettle. Come through to the house."

Chapter Eight

As the pilot announced the plane was beginning its descent into Dublin Airport, Conor's face did a funny thing. His lips made a smile, and he could feel his cheek muscles moving too. The smile stayed fixed on his face for quite some time. The smile was not confined to his lips, though; it came from his stomach, filling him up all the way through his entire body. He did remember this feeling of happiness and excitement, two feelings existing together. His sister, Marie, was meeting him at Arrivals. Before he knew it, the plane was safely on the runway. *The weather here in Dublin today is eighteen degrees and sunny. Thank you for flying with Dublin Airways today. Have a safe onward journey.*

***

Marie couldn't wait to see her big brother. He had not been home for so long. He didn't make it to her thirtieth birthday party as he had been busy with work. He would have loved it too. It was at Lalor's Bar. Everyone she loved was there, apart from Conor. Granny had drunk Uncle Jim under the table, and the music was incredible. Her mammy and daddy had hired a local band called The Whistlers. They played until 2 am and did not miss a beat. Everyone was dancing and singing to all the greats.

Conor was only home for a few days as he was starting a new job, he had said on the phone. Marie was going to make the most of every second. They would go straight round to see Mammy and Daddy, who just could not wait to see their son. Then, off to Lalor's Bar for a drink or two this evening. She was sure Tommy and Alice, who had owned the place for over thirty-five years, would be thrilled to see Conor too. He used to play his bodhrán drum there every Friday night before he left for university in England. She dearly hoped that Conor had brought his drum with him. He used to take it everywhere; it was like an extension of him.

She kept a watchful eye on the automatic doors in the Arrivals hall. Every time they opened, she stood to attention, searching for Conor's face in the crowd. She had seen on the Arrivals board that his flight had landed. She could hardly take the anticipation any longer, and it was making her stomach do flips. Finally, the doors parted, and among the faces, there he was, Conor, with his bodhrán drum case tied to the top of his backpack. She mirrored his growing smile as they moved towards each other through the other passengers. She squeezed him so tight, and he squeezed her right back.

"Well then," he said to her, "what do you know? How are you?"

"I'm grand," she said. "Welcome home."

They talked nonstop on the car journey and laughed — real belly laughs. They sang to the radio and just loved being in each other's company. As Marie drove round the square to their parents' home, Conor felt something he had not felt for a long time — relaxed and alive inside.

Their parents' home was a semi-detached, with two bedrooms upstairs and two sitting rooms downstairs. The sitting room at the back was where people arrived first, as the carport was there. It had the kitchen and the AGA. This was their mammy's sitting room. She was always having the neighbours round for a cuppa and a chat. The sitting room at the front was where Daddy had his naps on the sofa. And, as sure as can be, that is what they were doing when Conor came in round the back porch into his mammy's sitting room.

He could see his mammy had one of the neighbours round too. It was like a moment frozen in time. Just how he pictured his mammy when he thought of home. It was so heartwarming.

"Mammy," he called as he came in through the door, "I've missed you."

"Conor, you're home." She squeezed the life out of him and instructed Marie to get two more tea cups out of the press. "You're as handsome as ever," she said, repeatedly covering his face in kisses. "Now then," she said,
"sit yourself there and tell me everything."

His mammy and the neighbour, Carol, emptied the contents of the fridge onto the table in front of him. Slices of beef, homemade soda bread, butter, cheddar cheese, tomatoes grown by Daddy in his greenhouse and Daddy's famous giant spring onions, homemade scones, cream, jam – two flavours, blueberry and strawberry, both homemade by Carol. "Eat up, there's plenty more," says Mammy.

"Now then, Conor Simon," Daddy says as he enters the room, "where's my boy? What a sight. You look grand." He pulls Conor to his feet and embraces him.

"You too, Daddy, you too," says Conor. Then Mammy joins them, squeezing them tight.

"Now, let me look at ye," she says. They all sit down together, drinking tea and eating homemade, home-grown food all afternoon, laughing and joking like no time has passed. Conor told his family before he had arrived that he had been struggling. They sympathetically listened to what he had been going through.

"We love every inch of you," Mammy said, and they all agreed.

That evening, they all went for a drink at Lalor's Bar.

"A whiskey for Daddy, a tall Martini and lemonade for Mammy, a pint of Guinness for Conor, and a pint of Guinness for me," Marie said to Tommy at the bar. She reached over and took Conor's hand as they waited for the drinks order. "You'll always have a home here," she said to him.

"I know I do, and I also know what that means for me now," says Conor. "I have a home in County Laois and a home in Yorkshire. I have both." He kissed her forehead.

"Now then," called out Julia as she walked towards them, "where's that Conor Simon Murphy? Let me look at ye. A sight for sore eyes."

Tommy put the drinks down on the bar. He looked at Conor. "And that bodhrán drum, that's a grand sight too. Come on, Conor, don't keep us waiting," he said excitedly. "And Marie, you've your flute?"

"Yes, Tommy."

"Grand … grand," Julia said.

Then Tommy began his announcement: "Ladies and gentlemen, tonight for one night only, brother and sister duo — I give you the Murphy's."

The music sounded so great, and everyone sang along. The atmosphere was incredible, and all were enjoying themselves. Conor's parents were so proud of their children.

Conor had told them before he arrived that he had quit his job, and he was surprised at their reaction. They didn't care. He had thought him being a manager was what they were proud of, but Mammy and Daddy were just proud that he was their son. That was all he needed to be, nothing more.

"Well then," said Conor, "shall we play one of my favourites since I'm home, "Lovely Laois?" A whoop and a cheer from the crowd, banging feet on the floor. He took that as a "yes" and began playing.

On the second day of his visit, Conor knew exactly where he wanted to go — his childhood playground, the ruins of Dunstan Castle. He sat on the back wall, waiting for Marie to arrive. He heard her car coming before he saw it round the corner very carefully down the uniform road. He smiled a wide, full-bodied smile again as he saw her. He was like an excited twelve-year-old again.

"Hello," she had the window down, waving to him. It was a nice summer day again, not too hot. "Your carriage awaits," she joked. "Jump in." It was a short ten-minute journey as they grew up just at the other end of the town to where their parents live now. The castle speared in view as they ascended Dunstan Hill. Conor's mind filled with thoughts and memories that had not occupied the conscious part of it for many years. It was like an old film reel running in his head. He could see himself with his friends, sword in hand, well actually, stick, that he had found on the floor, in hand. Then there would be jousting. Now, they were galloping as if they were on horseback with the longest sticks they could find. And homemade slingshots like tiny little trebuchets to fling stones at the castle walls. Looking back, he was amazed that he, Fin and Niall had all emerged from childhood without broken bones or losing an eye! He fondly remembered his time playing here—the start of his adventures.

Conor and Marie reminisced about their childhood as they walked around the ruins, the white lichen clinging to what remained of the castle walls; nature was trying to claim back the land with overgrown grass, brambles and nettles.

Conor told Marie about the sleepwalking, the secret room and the key that Bobby, the blacksmith, had made. "Let's search this castle for secret rooms," she said, wide-eyed and excited. She left Conor standing there as she raced off on her quest. He laughed and ran after her. For a brief time, they were children again. They searched high and low and found stone openings that were perhaps once magnificent doors that needed enormous, heavy keys. Now, however, it was more a ruin than a castle. They could only use their imaginations now to see it as it was.

Eventually, they ran out of steam and sat on the grass in the centre of the ruin, laughing at each other childishly and slightly breathless.

"Are you okay?" Marie asked Conor.

"I'm getting there …" he said, "… slowly. We make cages for ourselves in life," he said philosophically, "or dungeons. Let's go dungeons, as we are sitting in a castle. Deep black dungeons. I built myself one. Brick by brick. The thing is, it never started out that way. I was just building a life for myself. It started out good. It was what I wanted. But, one day, I looked round, and I had changed, but I thought I

had to keep building. Then, I got stuck there, or rather, I thought I was stuck there, with my choices, forever. It's taken me a long time, but I realised that the door to the dungeon was always open. All I had to do was walk out, but because I'd invested so much of my life building it, I thought I had to stay there, that it was too late to start again. And it is harder because I'm not starting with a clean sheet. I'm starting with a crumpled, torn, scribbled-on sheet, but I can change it."

Marie nodded, following his train of thought and his analogies. "We've gone from castles to paper, but I think I understand you. The visit home and the new job, are they walking you out of the dungeons?"

"Yeah, you got it."

"Or un-creasing the paper," she said, and they both laughed, putting their arms around one another.

"Sword fight!" said Conor.

"Sword fight," said Marie.

"Ready, choose your weapon."

They both jumped to their feet, brushing the grass from their hands. They raced to pick the biggest twigs they could find to "fight to the death". Well, the death of their energy, anyway. Then, they headed back to their parents' home. On the way, they stopped for an ice cream at Conor's request.

***

As the time came to go home to Yorkshire from his home in Ireland, Conor embraced his family, including Carol, who was over for a cuppa and a chat with more strawberry jam. He gave them each a gift. He had commissioned Bobby to make them. They were small, iron lucky horseshoes with a shamrock pattern on one side. "I'll be back soon, for Christmas. I've already booked my ticket," he said.

"Come on, now," said Marie, "let's get you to the airport."

"Okay, okay. Bye, Mammy. Bye, Daddy. Bye, Carol."

"Now, would you take some jam and white pudding with you?" said Mammy, her eyes brimming.

"I've no room in my pack. Save it for me." He called back as he walked out the door, "Love yous."

"Love you," they called back.

"So, what's your new job?" asked Marie on the drive to the airport. "Is it some big mystery?"

"It just might well be," he said, winking at her. She shook her head and laughed. She was not going to get a straight answer out of him.

Chapter Nine

It was 8:00 am, and Conor was excited as today was the day he started his new job. He had a sage green polo shirt with one of those shiny badges with his name on. He looked good. He had an optional sage green fleece for the colder days and could style them with either trousers or shorts. He no longer had to wear tight-fitting suits on hot days or shine his shoes. In fact, if his shoes were not slightly dirty or very dirty at the end of his working day, he must have done something wrong.

The night he had done the audio tour at the abbey was when he saw the job advertisement on his way home. It was also the night he booked his plane ticket home. To Ireland.

Conor had a ten-minute walk to work. It was a beautiful autumn morning; the sun was shining with just a slight chill in the air—a perfect day to start his new job.

He was greeted by a friendly face, "Hi, good morning, Conor. So good to see you. Welcome."

"Good morning," said Conor to Lisa.

She smiled a big, wide smile and told him, "I'm going to be showing you the ropes today, and this here is Henry."

Henry looked up from the desk, "What cha," he said, "you all right?"

"Grand," said Conor.

"So, this is the ticket desk," said Lisa. "Henry is going to be working on it today. So, he'll greet the tourists and check their membership to see if they just want a day pass or if they might visit other historical sites while they're here in Yorkshire. Henry will also give out the audio tours. He'll give them a brief resumé of how they go around the site and a quick go over the buttons, on/off, play, etc. And me and you, kid, we will be doing the guided tour, giving them the full works. Are you ready, Conor?"

"I was born ready," said Conor. Just then, the first coach arrived in the car park.

"Looks like we're on," said Lisa. "Ah, welcome. Welcome, everyone, to Yorkshire and our historical abbey."

***

Conor had been working at the abbey for a couple of weeks, and he was really enjoying it. He had made the role his own, giving the visitors historical facts but also telling them ghost stories on the special ghost tours that were taking place now that the evenings were beginning to get darker again, heading into autumn.

Conor helped arrange a musical evening at the abbey with Aneesha, Sammy and Derrick. Conor was quite taken aback by how moving himself physically and changing his environment, first to Ireland and then into a new job, had helped him shift mentally too. Sometimes, though, he missed the comfort of his old routine. He found it strange that an environment he did not flourish in could also be something he missed. Like he had done it for so long, his brain had become wired to the routine — synapses firing down the same pathway every day, making stronger and stronger connections. So strong that it was now slightly uncomfortable that they were no longer needed as the new routines began to take their place.

Lisa was helping Conor set up. He walked over to meet her at the abbey museum as she locked up for the evening. She smiled as she saw him approaching.

"Ready to do this?" she called out to him.

"Oh yes, I'm ready, but the question is, Lisa, are you?" She snorted out a laugh and rolled her eyes at him.

Lisa had contacted the lighting crew she used at the Abbey Illuminations. They were already setting up. It was going to look amazing with the old ruins illuminated by coloured lights that would stretch up their walls into the night sky. Tones of blue slowly changing into purple, followed by red, then green and returning to blue to start the sequence again.

Lisa and Conor set the stage for himself and his fellow musicians. They would be at the centre of the cloister with the audience a full 360 degrees around them, where the walkway around the cloister would have been.

Conor could imagine the walls still in situ with people sitting in the arched window ledges to get a clear view of the centre of the cloisters. This is why it was such an extraordinary evening — different acoustics and a unique layout. A central stage. And space all the way up to the heavens, even in a crowd. Totally different to playing down the local pub. Conor felt nervous but mainly excited and thrilled to have this opportunity. It was not a raised stage; it didn't need to be in this location. It was a large piece of rubber flooring, creating a flat area over the grass. Each of them would have a microphone and special dynamic mics for their instruments to ensure everyone could hear.

Aneesha, Derrick and Sammy arrived to set up. Lisa and Conor greeted them with big smiles of excitement. There was a real sense of fun and good vibes, with everyone getting ready for the big event. There were still a couple of hours before the start of the concert, so they carried out a sound check, and after that, Conor went to freshen up.

The four musicians took to the stage. It was dark now, and the lighting setup looked amazing. Conor had never seen so many people at the abbey. They entered the cloister to a round of applause. Each of them took their positions and their instruments in hand. Sammy, poised with the viola to her chin, bow in hand, placed gently on the strings as if holding a yoga position, so still and strong. Aneesha, her flute held to her lips, arms strong and fingers posed. Derrick, with his tin whistle held in a relaxed position in both hands, ready to lift on cue, a big, relaxed smile on his face, stretching from ear to ear. Then Conor, holding his bodhrán drum in his left hand, stick held loosely in the middle like you would hold a pen, turned in towards his body and held up by his chin, heart beating fast, but in a good way. Then they began. The drum first. Then the tin whistle, beautiful music reverberating around the open space. Then, together, perfectly in sync, the flute and the viola. What an evening. Conor never could have imagined, just a few short months ago, that any of this would have been possible.

He was immensely happy, but he also had a ball of dread and doubt deep in the pit of his stomach. It was like a residual piece of the anxiety and depression, not enough to ruin the evening but just enough to remind him that it was still there in some small way. Still part of him now. He was snapped out of his thoughts by the reaction of the crowd. The adoration boosted his feel-good chemicals and shut down the negative thoughts, stopping them in their tracks. As the applause went on, he felt appreciated, purposeful. If only he could bottle this feeling for himself and for others too. Derrick put his hand up in the air, signalling an imminent high-five, so Conor lifted his hand too. Then Aneesha and Sammy joined. It was an evening to remember.

***

A week had passed since the big music night. Everyone agreed it had been a great success. Conor was at work. He walked along whistling and singing unconsciously. He was naturally cheerful, enjoying his work. He was making his way over to the main entrance to greet another group who had signed up for the guided tour of the abbey.

"Good afternoon and welcome to James Bridge Abbey. You're very welcome here today.

There's a little chill in the air but still a fine, bright day. I'm Conor. As you can tell by my accent, I have not always lived in James Bridge, though I now consider myself a local." The group chuckled, already impressed by Conor's natural performance talents. "Shall we begin?" He led them into the abbey grounds. It had been easy for him to learn the tour script as he already knew so much about the abbey. He knew all the historical facts, but he didn't just reel them off in a list, he gave an enthusiastic and informative tour. He gave value for money. The visitors especially enjoyed finding out about the discovery of the ceramic tiles off the library. He, of course, had first-hand expertise to share of their discovery. As Conor settled into his new routine, he felt good. He was now beginning to carve a job, a role, a life, with himself at the centre rather than pushing himself, fitting into roles and spaces he simply could not merely exist in. Conor was excited by the abbey. He saw it as a living entity, always changing and surprising, always giving a bit more and always providing new experiences.

***

Conor awoke. It was a dark winter morning. He picked up his phone to check the time. He guessed what time he thought it was before looking: *7.40 am*. Then he looked down at his phone. He smiled a little, satisfied with himself that he was so close; it was 7.42. His alarm was due to go off at 7.45, so he enjoyed snuggling back into his blankets, cosy and warm.

He much preferred his abbey uniform over his old manager's suit. He had prepared his clothes as usual, the sage green polo shirt hanging on the back of the door, his favourite breakfast cereal, pineapple granola and a bowl set out on the table. Conor took a quick shower, dressed and then ate breakfast. He put his bowl and cup in the dishwasher, wiped down the table and put on his shoes. He still had some of his old routines, but his work life was quite different now. He grabbed his black winter coat, the one with the thermal lining and fluffy hood, from the hook by the door and headed out to work.

It was Conor's last day at work before they broke up for Christmas. He had two weeks off over the festive period and was heading home to Ireland. He locked up the museum and wished Lisa and Henry a merry Christmas, and that was him done for two whole weeks. He walked home, running through a checklist in his head. He was heading straight to the airport. He had packed his bag before work but wanted to check he had everything: Christmas presents, passport, drum, wash bag, charger. By the time he got home, he was satisfied he had everything. *Half an hour before the taxi arrives.* He had a quick shower, changed, and had five minutes to spare. He sat looking out the window. He was really looking forward to his first Christmas at home for a long time. Beep Beep. The taxi was here.

***

Marie drove round the back of the square and parked in the carport. Conor had been so pleased to see her at the airport, and now he could not wait to see his mammy and daddy. They went in through the back door, and there was Mammy, ready to embrace him.
"Happy Christmas, love." She threw her arms round him.

Daddy came in. He had been hanging lights outside at the front, and now the whole house was ready for Christmas. Daddy joined in the embrace and pulled Marie in too.   Tinsel was strung on the walls, coloured fairy lights blinking in the window, and half a dozen novelty Christmas characters were dotted around the room: the ones that dance and sing and wiggle and wish you a merry Christmas.

There was a tree in both the rooms, front and back.

"Hang on," said Conor. "You're not quite ready; one more thing." He went to his bag dropped by the back door. "Hang on, they're here somewhere." He rooted around in his large backpack. "Here," he said and pulled out a carrier bag.

"What on earth is it?" said Mammy. "You'll see," he said. Inside the bag were three rectangular gift boxes. He gave one to each of them. "Go on, then, open them," said Conor. "Together!" he added.

"Exciting," said Marie.

"Now? Before Christmas?" said Mammy.

"Yes, yes, it's for the tree," Conor said. "Come on, then. What are we waiting for," said Daddy.

They each opened their box. A beautifully crafted magical Santa key, made by Bobby, of course. Each with a golden ribbon to hang on the tree, a name tag, and a little jingly sleigh bell.

Marie beamed as she took it out. "How thoughtful," she said, hugging Conor.

"Now Santa can open the door to bring all the presents in. Thank you," said Daddy.

Conor looked at Mammy. She had gone rather quiet. She held the box open in her hand, staring down at her key. She had a tear in her eye. "Do you like it, Mammy?" Conor asked. Mammy shut the box and ran upstairs, crying. Conor was shocked. That was not the reaction he was expecting. Marie looked at Daddy.

"What's wrong, Daddy? Should I go up and see?"

"No, I'll go," he said. And with that, he disappeared upstairs, leaving Marie and Conor in silence for a moment, unsure what had just happened.

Marie looked at Conor sympathetically, saying, "It's a lovely gift."

"Why did it upset Mammy?" he asked. "I've no idea. Maybe we should put the kettle on and wait for Daddy to talk to her?" Marie popped the kettle on the AGA, and Conor took the cups and the teapot out of the press, ready. They sat in silence until the kettle whistled. The door opened, and Daddy entered.

"Conor, Mammy wants to see you upstairs." He looked serious and concerned. Conor wondered what could be going on. How could his return for Christmas and handing out gifts have turned from merriment to concern so quickly? He did as he was asked and went upstairs to see Mammy. The third step creaked and signalled him coming. On the walls of the stairway was a gallery of pictures. Marie and him as kids, on a holiday somewhere he could not recall. School photographs. One of him, aged eight, with his front tooth missing. His graduation photo with him in his cap and gown. One of Mammy, Daddy and Marie at Marie's 30th birthday. He really liked that one. *I should ask for a copy.* He pushed open the door of Mammy and Daddy's bedroom. "Mammy?" he said gently. She was sitting on the end of her bed.

"Come in, love. Sit down." She patted the bed next to her. He sat down.

"Are you okay, Mammy? Did I upset you with the gift? I'm sorry."

"Yes, you did, but it is not you who should be sorry, it should be me. I didn't mean for so many years to pass by. I really didn't. Your daddy too. He always thought you should know, but you were so little. How could we have told you?"

"Told me what, Mammy?"

"Well, I wanted to be the one to tell you, and now it's maybe thirty years too late. I hope you can forgive me for keeping it from you for so long. I just wanted you to be happy."

"What is it, Mammy? You're scaring me."

"I want to tell you. I always have. I just don't know how to get the words out."

"Just try, please, Mammy. Go on."

118

"A long time ago, when I was a young woman, I met a man and fell in love with him."

"Before Daddy?"

"Yes, before Daddy." She paused and inhaled, blowing all the way out through her mouth. "Oh, dear Jesus, I hope you still love me after this."

"Mammy, I love you." He reassured her.

"I fell pregnant." She looked away from Conor's gaze. He held her hand and squeezed it to encourage her to continue. "Before I could tell Simon – that was his name – he was in a road accident, and he died." Conor's eyes widened.

"How awful." But he needed to know where she was leading with all this information he had never heard before. "Did you decide not to have the baby, Mammy? Is that what you're trying to tell me? It's okay."

She looked him straight in the eyes and held his hands tightly. "I had the baby, darling. Best thing I ever did."

The pieces were beginning to land in his mind, but he needed her to say it, as it was like he was having an out-of-body experience and this was happening to someone else. "I'm the baby?" he asked her.

"Yes, you're the baby, my darling boy. You're my baby."

He froze, a million thoughts jumping in and out of his mind. He realised he was holding his breath, so he exhaled. Mammy waited for a response. "Daddy," he said.

"I started dating Daddy when I was seven months pregnant," she answered. "We were just friends at first, but he soon became my everything. He was amazing, and he loved you from the minute you were born." Conor began to cry. He loved his daddy. Mammy cried too.

"Does Marie know?" Mammy shook her head. "And Marie is Daddy's?" She nodded between her sobs. "I need a minute," Conor said, letting go of his mammy's hand. He stood up and backed towards the door. "I need a minute," he said again. "I'll be back." He walked down the stairs and straight out of the front door.

***

Marie and Daddy heard the front door shut. They shared a look. One that said, what should we do? They instinctively knew it was Conor who had left the house.

"I'll go see Mammy," said Daddy.

"I'll go see Conor."

"Just hold on now, love. Just wait. Let me see Mammy first. We need to talk to you." With that, he left the back sitting room and went upstairs. Marie was left sitting on her own, watching the fairy lights twinkle, wondering what on earth just happened. She began to feel panicked. She had a tingling, burning sensation on the palm of her hands and into her fingers. She was clenching her jaw, and her heart was beating quicker than normal, pulsing in her ears. She stood up to make the tea but was frozen to the spot, so she sat back down. She twirled her mass of black curls like she used to when she was a little girl. After what felt like an eternity, she heard footsteps on the stairs. She was reluctant to find out what was going on as it could not be good. At the same time, she was desperate to know.

Mammy had been crying, she could see, and Daddy looked concerned. Daddy came in and put his hand on the kettle to see if it was still hot. Mammy pulled up a chair close to Marie, facing her and took her hands in hers. Daddy put the kettle back on the heat. "Now then. I told Conor something I should have told him and you, my darling Marie, years ago, but I never found the words or the right moment." Marie was worried now, and her mind raced as she waited for her mammy to say more. "I've told him that before Daddy, there was another man in my life. A man I met and started a relationship with, but he died in a road accident."

Marie was sad at this revelation, but she was still unsure where Mammy was going with this. "What does this have to do with Conor Simon?"

"When he died, I was pregnant. Pregnant with Conor." Marie looked at Mammy, then at Daddy. Tears started to form in her blue eyes. Daddy lifted the kettle, which had started to whistle off the heat and filled the teapot.

"But…" That's the one word she managed. While Daddy poured the tea, Mammy continued.

"I was seven months gone when I started dating your Daddy. We were great friends at first, but it wasn't long until we fell in love." She turned to smile at Daddy as he brought the tea over. Daddy sat down with them. He held Mammy's hand and squeezed it. He turned to Marie and placed his arm around her.

"We're still a family," he said.

"But why did you never tell us?" asked Marie.

"It was too hard at first for Mammy. She'd already been through it. The grief, the pregnancy, and she was still so young, barely twenty-one. Then there was me, Mammy and Conor. A young family. Trying to adjust."

Mammy interjected, "Babies are hard work, love. Beautiful, but hard work, and I don't know what I would have done without Daddy." Daddy continued. "Simon, that was Conor's biological father's name."

"You named him after him. His middle name – Simon." Marie said.

Mammy nodded. "I had so many conflicting emotions," she said. "I had loved Simon, but it was brief, a first love; we had known each other less than a year before his accident. The grief was not only for him but for Conor not to know his father. Then, Eoin, my darling," she said, returning the hand squeeze. "Eoin was in my life. We knew each other in passing, from school, and sometimes we played darts in Lalor's Bar. We spent more and more time together. It happened so easily in such a turbulent time. It was true love. Daddy was there for Conor from the moment he was born. He was a natural father. We grew together as a family, and things were really good. Conor was so content and happy as a young child. He had such a grand relationship with Daddy that it seemed unfair to tell him; it never felt like the right moment. As the years passed, it seemed to matter less and less that he should know. But I was wrong. I should have told him. And now that I have, I hope he can forgive me."

Chapter Ten

Conor wandered the streets of his home town.
In the darkness and rain, he plodded up and
down alleys he used to play in as a child. He
walked past the sweetshop on the corner of the
main road that still sold pick-and-mix sweets —
jars and jars of cola cubes, bonbons – strawberry
or lemon – midget gems, pear drops, Yorkshire
mixture, dolly mixtures, boiled aniseed,
liquorice, white chocolate mice. It was closed,
but Conor Simon could see through the lit-up
shop window. Childhood memories rushed in
of receiving his pocket money for helping out at
the bog, collecting turf for fuel during the winter
and piling it up in the back shed. He would then
walk straight to this very sweet shop and spend
every penny on sweets. He was allowed to. His
daddy always said: "It's up to you. You earned
it, it's your money. You can save it for
something you want, or you can spend it all on
sweets." Of course, a ten-year-old Conor Simon
spent it all on sweets. *Daddy*, he thought, *My
daddy*. The one that was all he knew, everything
he remembered, but it was like his memories
had all shifted like there was a shadow looming
over them. They had altered now. *Daddy*, he
thought, but he's not. Not *my* daddy. Tears
formed in his eyes as he tried to process this
new reality. He felt like he was still his daddy,

Eoin Murphy. He even had his surname. He wondered if anyone else knew. His mum's sister, Julia? She must know, surely. Had she kept the secret too?   He caught his reflection in the shop window, and his thoughts jumped again. He wondered what his biological dad looked like. He wondered if he looked like him. Then he thought of his daddy again. He had never considered that he didn't look like his daddy's son. Most people had said he looked more like Mammy, but no one had ever questioned that he was not Daddy's. Or at least not that he knew of. Nor to his face. Then, his thoughts turned to Marie. He had just left the house when he found out. Did she know what was going on? Would she still love him the same now that they were only half-siblings? Then he wondered if it was possible that he had any other siblings on his biological father's side. Mammy said she was very young. Was he young too. It occurred to him that he did not know anything about his biological father other than his name, Simon. He had not stuck around long enough for Mammy to tell him anymore. She had named him after him. Why? Then, another question dawned on him. Why today? Mammy hadn't given him one clue, not one conversation, but today, he had barely been through the door ten minutes, and for some reason, she decided today was the day to tell him.

Then, he remembered that she had just opened the gift he had brought home for the Christmas tree, the Santa keys that Bobby made, and then she ran off upstairs crying. Why? He puzzled again. His head was hurting. He felt like he would not get any peace of mind until some of his questions were answered. He knew he needed to go home for the answers, and he would, but not yet. He wasn't ready.

Drops of water trickled down his face, his short black hair wet from the rain. The rain was solace for him. The physical sensations helped him still feel present in his body when his head was filled with unanswered questions and puzzles. The rain and the darkness meant that the streets were quiet. It gave him physical space to be alone with his thoughts and emotions. It was not the day he imagined or the welcome home he had predicted.

It was late when Conor finally returned. Marie had gone home, and Mammy and Daddy had gone to bed. He found his backpack in the spare room. His bed was freshly made up, a towel on the end and a mint chocolate on his pillow. Mammy had done this, he knew. It was like staying in a hotel. There was a note next to the bedside table from Daddy. It simply said I love you, son. *I love you too, Daddy*, he thought.

He took off his wet clothes and placed them over the clothes horse. He used the towel to dry his hair. He found his wash bag and got ready for bed. He didn't think he could sleep, but within five minutes of laying his head on the pillow, he was fast asleep, exhausted by the day.

When he woke the next morning, he could hear Marie talking to Mammy and Daddy in hushed tones. Either they were trying not to wake him, or they were talking about him, or maybe both. His eyes felt sore and sleepy, his body heavy. He wondered if things would be better if Mammy hadn't told him yesterday. Then, he wondered if it would have been better to tell him as a child. How would a small child have felt receiving the news? Maybe there was never a 'right time'. He decided to put a pin in his thoughts. He was so tired and so hungry. He hadn't eaten since he arrived yesterday. *Breakfast*, he thought. *Let's start the day there and take it as it comes.*

He did not own a dressing gown or slippers at home in Yorkshire, but the last time he came home, Mammy bought him some for when he stayed. He put them on and headed down the stairs. As he walked into the back room, Mammy, Daddy and Marie all stopped what they were doing and looked at him in silence. "Morning," Conor said quite casually, which seemed to throw them.

127

"Morning, son," said Daddy first.

"Morning," said Marie and Mammy together.

"You hungry, love?" asked Mammy.

"I could eat the back door covered in butter," he replied. Mammy seemed happy with this response and filled a plate with sausage, bacon, black pudding, tomatoes and fried eggs. She served it with two slices of soda bread and strong, milky tea. Conor would have coffee at home in Yorkshire, but this cuppa tasted great. Everyone joined Conor at the table with their cups of tea in hand. Mammy placed the teapot in the centre in case anyone wanted a top up. Conor looked up from devouring his breakfast and realised everyone was looking at him.

"Did you sleep much?" Marie asked him.

"Like a log," he said.

"Oh," she seemed surprised, "I didn't." Mammy and Daddy looked tired too.   "How are you feeling this morning?" asked Daddy. Simon took a bite of his heavilybuttered soda bread and paused to think about the question.

"Hmm," he said, "okay. Still trying to process it all, but I'm sitting here with my mammy, my daddy and my sister. You know what I mean? That, at its core, it's the same. I now have another biological father, and I have lots of questions." He looked at Mammy, and she nodded.

"We are brother and sister, always," said Marie in tears, and she reached her hand across the table to his. Mammy then started crying too. "I'm so sorry I had kept the truth from you." She stood up and held him tightly around his shoulders. Conor looked towards Daddy to see him tearing up too. Eoin stood up and threw his arms around them, too, joining in the embrace. Conor smiled. *My crazy, loving family*, he thought.

"I love you, too, guys, but there is one thing.

"Yes?" said Marie tentatively.

"Can I finish my fry up now, please?" They all laughed and let go.

"Shall we go for a walk after breakfast, Mammy?" he asked. "Just you and me?"

"Yes," Mammy answered, "let's." Conor and Mammy set off walking. "Walk down to the duck pond, should we?" asked Conor.

"Yes," said Mammy. It was a cold, crisp morning but fine and dry. "Ask me anything you like," she said.

"Why did my gift upset you? Had you planned to tell me now? It was like it sparked a reaction in you."

"A memory," she answered. "It sparked a memory."

"Of Simon?"

"Yes, of Simon. Simon was the groundskeeper for Dunstan Castle. Oh, he loved that job, he did. It's the perfect job for me, he used to say. He loved working outdoors, and he loved the history of the place. He took me on our first date there. A picnic in the middle of the castle grounds. It was very romantic.

"He told me the derelict remains of this once magnificent sixteenth-century stronghold suffered considerable damage in 1652 when it was attacked by Cromwellian forces during the War of the Three Kingdoms. He seemed so knowledgeable to me; I could have listened to him talk all day. Being the groundskeeper, he used to joke that he had the keys to the castle. He used to wear them on a key chain hooked onto his belt loop. One was for the storage area where the garden equipment was kept, one was for the toilets on site, one was for the blocked-off staircase as they were too corroded to climb, and one for the dungeons! He used to laugh. I'm not actually sure if he really did have the key for the dungeons or not." She smiled at this memory.

Conor did not interject at any point as he was so absorbed in her stories and wanted to know more. He was trying to take it all in.

"We had been dating for around three months, and it was Christmas. Simon gave me a gift. In a little rectangular gift box with a golden ribbon tied around it. It was a key, a chunky iron key, and he had written inside the box, *The keys to the castle for my Queen*." A tear rolled down her cheek, and she wiped it away. "I had been thinking about telling you for a while. I thought you were living a happy life in Yorkshire, and I didn't want to spoil that, so I didn't think you needed to know. And I wasn't going to tell you over the phone all those miles apart from you. But when you came home, you opened up about your depression and not fitting into your life anymore. I felt you needed to know. So, yes, I had planned to tell you, but not there and then on the spot when you had just walked through the door. The key triggered the memory and was such a beautiful gift in so many ways. I just could not believe that nearly four decades on, there you were standing there in front of me, giving me the same gift. I knew then one hundred per cent that I could not hold it back from you any longer. It was like a sign. Like the two of you are connected. Now you even have a very similar job and interest in history. I cannot describe how that felt. It took me back all those years to that twenty-one-year-old me.

"How could I keep it from you any longer? I just hope you can forgive me and Daddy for keeping it from you. It was what I wanted, and he respected that. He supported me and you, fully. He loved us unconditionally then and now. I thought that would be enough, but I see now you do have a connection with Simon. Although you never met him, he's in here." She stopped walking and put her hand over his heart.

Conor Simon hugged her tight. "How can I be cross with you, Mammy? You're such a beautiful person. You did what you thought was best. It's just going to take time to absorb it all and adjust. It's shaken my world upside down. I don't know how I feel. We will just have to take it step-by-step as a family." They kept walking. When they reached the duck pond, they found a bench facing the water. They sat close together to keep warm.

"Simon! You gave me his name?"

"Yes. Conor after my grandad and Simon after, well, after Simon, your biological father. Is that how I should refer to him now? Is that okay?"

"Let's just say Simon."

"It made sense at the time, and I guess it makes sense again, now that you know."

They sat in silence for a few minutes, staring at the water. "Bread!" Mammy said suddenly. Conor looked at her, puzzled. "For the mallards. We should have brought them some bread."

Conor laughed, then said, "You don't give ducks bread, Mammy. It's bad for them. You can give them special duck food, seeds and that dried sweetcorn."

"Well, they've always liked the bread."

"They might like it, Mammy, but that doesn't mean they should be eating it, now, does it?" Conor paused, then, "Do I look like him, Mammy?"

"Sometimes you do remind me of him. It's the black hair."

"He had black hair?"

"Yes, and green eyes. But you got my brown eyes."

"Do you have a picture of him?"

"Yes, a few. I'll get them out for you later."

"And his family? Do they still live nearby? Did they know about me?"

"No, his parents moved shortly after they lost Simon. I lost track of them. It's not like now with all your social media, smartphones and all that. He had a brother, Patrick. I only met him once. I think he was two years younger. He moved with his parents."

***

133

In and out, in and out of the ruined stone walls. The waxing moon in the sky above calls every molecule in Conor's body to action. In and out, his skin bubbling, his nervous system in full swing. Conor was lost in his head and in his thoughts. So much love for his Mammy and Daddy but so much anger too. So much understanding for a young twenty-one-year-old Myra, but also resentment for keeping such a secret from him all his life. He was unable to focus on any of his majestic surroundings — the ruins of Dunstan Castle. He had come here to feel closer to his biological father.

He became more present, feeling the cold night air. He imagined Simon working here all year round. The dramatic outline towered up to the moon as though crying out from a past long distant but not wholly gone, somehow still present there in the existing remains. It seemed to bring back memories of his father, but they were just imagined memories.

He pictured Simon walking across the grounds in front of him, his keys hooked on his belt. He could hear them jangle. The lumbering stone walls of the castle become the setting for conjuring his father's ghost memory, lit by the waxing gibbous moon, soon to become the winter's cold, full moon. The winter solstice, the longest night of the year, heralded the final season again in the Northern Hemisphere.

How much he had changed since a year ago. He let his feelings sit side-by-side, and he allowed himself to feel them slowly without judgement. He did not want to feel angry or let down by his parents, but he did. That is why he had come for a walk on his own, to let the earlier conversations of the day digest.

His mind was filled with the parallels between himself and his father, which made him feel like he knew him somehow. He wished he could meet with him, have a conversation with him. Look him in the eyes. How would he ever be anything more than just an imagining, not even a memory? It was the strangest feeling. He took his phone out of his pocket and dialled Marie. It was getting late, but she answered straight away. "I've been waiting for you to call me," she said.

"Come and meet me?" he asked.

"Yes, where?"

"At the castle."

"Give me ten minutes, and I'll be there."

Conor walked around in the darkness, following the ghost of his unknown father as he tended the grounds of the castle. He was willing him into existence. Never going to happen. He went up to the road to wait for Marie.
Eventually, he saw her headlights approaching. She wrapped her long scarf around her neck and

put her bobble hat on before getting out of the car.

"Let's walk," Conor said to her.

"Okay, let's walk. How are ye?" she asked. "Or is that a silly question? I can only imagine how you'd be. I feel like my world has been rocked, and I've not found out I have a different father to the one I've always known." Conor felt guilty that it had not until now crossed his mind to consider how Marie must be feeling after the revelation.

"Marie," he said, "I'm sorry."

"Whatever for?"

"I just went off on my own without speaking to you when I found out."

"You're speaking to me now, aren't ye? Mammy told me he used to work here. Simon. Your daddy. That sounds weird. Our daddy, Eoin, is Daddy."

"Simon. Let's just say Simon. Okay. I want to find him." Marie looked at him, confused. "I mean, I know I can't, but I want to. It's like everything has changed, but then nothing at all, and I now just carry on as before because it's not like I can have a relationship with him. So, what am I to do with this new information? Nothing?"

"You can't meet your daddy, I mean Simon, but you can meet his family. Didn't

Mammy say Simon had a brother?"

"Yes, Patrick."

"Let's find him, then."

***

Conor and Daddy sat in Lalor's Bar at a corner table away from the main thoroughfare of the bar area. It was Christmas Eve, and Eoin had brought Conor out of the house for a one-to-one chat as the past week had been so hectic and fraught. Conor Simon had spent so much time with Myra, trying to gather as much information as she could remember about Simon. Then he and Marie had been on the Internet, joining Irish ancestors' groups and researching the best DNA testing kits to order.

Eoin felt he had not had any quality time with his son to check in with him. Eoin was supportive of Conor. He had known the circumstances from day one when he had met Myra. He knew that even though Conor could never meet Simon, he would inevitably be connected to him on some level. He had always just supported Myra and her choices. He did not want to hide away in the background like an unwanted visitor or a redundant parent. He did not want Conor to feel in any way that he was hurting him by doing this, so he had decided to be proactive in helping Conor find Simon's family. It would keep their bond strong, he hoped.

They were drinking whiskey, Daddy's drink of choice to warm him up on a cold winter's day. It was Christmas Eve, after all.

"Daddy," said Conor, "I want you to know that you will always be my father. When I think of it all from your point of view, I'm so proud to be your son. The way you supported Mammy and me. You know that, right?"

"Yes, of course. I want you to know I understand you needing to do this. I'll support you with whatever you need."

Eoin raised his glass of whiskey. He looked at Conor with a smile and said, "To us." Conor raised his glass to meet Daddy's, clinking them together. "To us."

"Now, what do you suppose Mammy will be having us doing when we get back home? I'm guessing you'll be peeling the potatoes, and I'll get the sprouts. One more for the road?"

"Yep, last one, then off home to prep the Christmas dinner. It's making me hungry thinking about it. The turkey!"

"The stuffing."

"The gravy."

"The cranberry sauce."

"The roast potatoes."

"The pigs in blankets."

"The Christmas pudding."

"The custard."

"It's so nice to be home with my family for Christmas and not working this year. I am glad we decided to have a quiet one—just me, you, Mammy and Marie."

When they'd finished, they stepped outside to a beautiful glistening layer of pure white virgin snow. They stopped in the doorway and looked up to watch the snowflakes float gently down to the ground underneath the street lights. They linked arms and stepped out into the snow, making footprints all the way home. Daddy's and Conor's footprints in the fresh snow, side-by-side.

***

Mammy was awfully quiet. When Conor asked if she was okay, she smiled and, without looking up, said, "Yes, yes, I just want everything to be perfect. Now, set those cranberries to cool down and, be a dear, and put the kettle on." She busied herself, grating the stale bread for the homemade stuffing. When the tea was ready, he insisted Mammy sit down for five minutes. She reluctantly agreed. She seemed distracted, distant, sad, even.

"You okay, Mammy?" he asked again.

"Yes, love. Are you?" She deflected. "Yes, I am, Mammy, and I want you to be too." She finally looked up towards him, patted his hand, and smiled a half dimple to try and reassure him. She looked tired like a lifetime of keeping secrets had had an untold effect on her whole being.

"Is there anything you want to talk about, Mammy?"

She paused, then, "Nope, come on, this Christmas dinner won't get ready itself." With that, she stood up again.

Conor had thought she had something on her mind, something she still had to say, to tell him. But maybe he had read it wrong.

The kitchen smelt amazing, and he looked forward to eating the food. A real homemade Christmas dinner, for the first time in years, so he let the feeling go and did not ask Mammy again. He, Mammy, Daddy and Marie had a lovely, quiet family Christmas and ate and ate until they could eat no more.

Chapter Eleven

Thirty Nine Years Previously

"Myra, are you going out tonight, darling, or would you like some of the beef stew I'm making?"

"Smells good, Mammy, but I'm going out with Simon."

Mammy smiled. "Oh yes, Simon."

"Mammy, stop teasing," Myra said.

"You two have been courting nearly a year now. Will he ask you to marry him soon?"

"Mammy!" Myra shook her head. She kissed her mammy on the head and said, "See you."

"Bye, darling."

Myra met Simon at their usual spot just along the street from the castle walls. It was a warm September evening, and they had planned to get fish and chips from O'Neil's chip shop and then walk down to the duck pond. Myra was there first. She could smell the fish and chips right down the road and began feeling hungry. She looked at her watch. He was only ten minutes late, but usually, he would be there waiting for her when she arrived. Myra sat on the wall. She swung her feet gently, kicking her heels into the stone, her long summer dress flowing with the movement.

Five minutes later, she could see Simon in the distance walking down the road. She felt excited to see him. She smiled and waved at him, carefully jumping down from the wall. Simon approached her, and almost instantly, she could tell something wrong with him. He was agitated and didn't greet her in his usual, loving, charming way. This jarred with Myra as she had never seen Simon this way before and was unsure how to react to him. "Hello," she said.

"Hi, Myra."

"Good day?"

"Not really."

"Are you hungry? The fish and chips smell great."

"No. Listen, I just need to go do a job first."

"Okay, I'll come with you. We can always eat later."

Simon did not seem too pleased at her suggestion to come with him. He neither agreed nor disagreed., He just started walking down the street, so she followed him. He was moving faster and faster until she was nearly running to keep his pace.

"Where are we going?" she asked.

"Erm, Shivey Street."

"Shivey Street? To do what?"

"A job."

"Yes, you already said that."

She followed after him, still none the wiser about the nature of the 'job'. Her tummy rumbled as they passed O'Neil's.

This half-walking half-running continued for a further ten minutes until they reached Shivey Street. Simon went into number twelve and told her to wait outside.

Myra had been waiting outside for half an hour, becoming more and more anxious about the mystery of what Simon was doing and why he was acting so strange. She looked at her watch. The chip shop would be closing soon. I should have had some of Mammy's stew, she thought as her stomach rumbled. She crossed her arms over her body, drumming her fingers on her arm. How long should she wait? Should she go in? Simon was pretty firm when he had told her to stay outside. What on earth was he doing in there? Another half an hour passed. The sun was setting, and Myra had just decided to leave when Simon appeared out of number twelve.

"Shall we go for a drink?" he said to her. Not, *sorry for keeping you waiting* or *that took longer than I thought*. Nothing. Again, she was following him, walking down the street and into Lalor's Bar. It was Friday night, and it was just about as busy as it ever gets. She tried to ask him what he had been doing, but the music and the humdrum of people made it nearly impossible

to have a conversation. "Usual?" he asked her. She nodded.

"A pint of Guinness and a Babycham, thanks."

He turned and smiled at her, seeming more relaxed now. She smiled back, still unsure of what she was feeling other than hungry. She tapped him on the shoulder.

"And a packet of Taytos."

"And a packet of Taytos," Simon added to the order.

They squeezed into a spot, standing at the end of the bar as there was nowhere to sit. Myra ate her Taytos and took a drink of her Babycham. As she did so, Simon downed his pint in one and signalled that he would get another.

At the bar, she could see him talking to someone she didn't recognise. When they finished their conversation, they shook hands, and Simon came back to Myra at the end of the bar.

144

"Who is it?" she asked.

"Aw, that's Patrick, so it is, my younger brother."

"Your brother?" Myra was surprised as they had been dating for eleven months, and Simon had never mentioned that he had a brother. "Your brother?"

"Well, my half-brother, really."

"Would you not introduce him?"

"Sure, next time. He's gone now."

"How come you've not mentioned Patrick before?"

"Well, he was in prison. He's just been out a few weeks, so I wasn't exactly in a rush to introduce you. Sorry."

"It's okay. Can I ask what he was in prison for?"

"Theft and assault."

"Oh."

"He's always had a way of finding trouble that one. Or if not, trouble finds him." "Was the job something to do with Patrick?"

"It was. He might need a hand later too." Simon finished another pint. "Another?" He nodded towards Myra's empty glass.

"Yes, please."

Simon's answers had left Myra with more questions. A brother. A brother that had been in jail. A job for him. She hoped Simon was not getting himself into any trouble or danger. Would Mammy be so happy if he proposed now that he was related to a criminal, she wondered.

Simon brought the drinks over. "You must be hungry," he said to Myra. "We never got fish and chips. I'm sorry."

Just then, Patrick appeared behind Simon.

"Maybe you'll get to introduced him to me tonight after all." Myra nodded in Patrick's direction.

Simon turned round. It was then they both realised Patrick had a cut on the side of his head, and blood was running down his face. Simon grabbed Patrick's arm, and they both headed to the door without saying a word to Myra. She followed them, pushing past the crowd at the bar. She stood outside on the doorstep, looking up and down the street, trying to see where they had gone. She could see a man walking up the middle of the road. He was staggering. Then, from the opposite direction, she saw headlights and heard an engine revving. She waved to the man to get out of the road. "Hey," she shouted. "Hey, you, get out of the road." The car was heading towards him. She waved her hands in warning at the car as it sped towards them. The driver took no notice, but he had seen the man. He was looking right at him, as was his passenger. She could not believe what she was seeing. They were heading towards the man at speed on purpose. It happened so quickly. They hit him. He flew up into the air and landed on the road. She felt sick. Then she could see reverse lights. A crowd of people rushed out of the pub at the noise to see what was happening. Myra and twenty-seven other witnesses watched the driver reverse over the man on the road and then drive off. This was followed by commotion as people shot into action. Somebody screamed.

Two men ran over to the figure lying on the road, quickly followed by a woman who said she was a nurse. A couple ran inside to call an ambulance and the Garda. Three men ran down the road after the car. More people came out of the pub. Myra just stood there, rooted to the spot. She began to shake and dropped down to her knees. "Are you okay?" Someone asked her. She shook her head. She could not speak from the shock. No, she was not okay. She did not know if she would ever be okay again. How could she be when she had just watched her boyfriend run a man over and leave him for dead?

"He's dead!" she heard someone say. And Myra's whole world had been shattered. Two weeks later, she discovered she was pregnant, and Simon was a murderer. Only Myra and her mammy knew the truth about the baby's father. Conor Simon's father. Myra would not have got through any of it without her mammy.

Then, six months later, Myra met Eoin. The most beautiful man in the world. What was she supposed to tell him? Who would want to raise a murderer's child? She did not want to lie. So many times, she had been so close to telling him, but she did not want him to treat or judge Conor Simon by his murderous father. She never wanted that for her child. He deserved a loving father. It was for this same reason she had never told Conor. She did not want him to judge himself or think he was in any way going to grow up to be like his dad. She had named him Conor Simon, too, as Eoin was expecting her to in memory of his dead father, tragically killed in a road accident. That's what she had told him. And the nights she had cried, Eoin had held her in her grief. She hated it at first; she thought that by giving Simon as a middle name, no one would ever use it, but the opposite had happened.

Out of deep love, respect and understanding, Eoin always used it. Then, others began to do the same, and it stuck. Her whole life since she was twenty-one had been a lie. More than a lie. It was a whole web of lies.

One lie to cover another, and she was still doing it, and it was taking its toll. She had considered telling Conor, but what good would come of it? What was the point of protecting him from the truth all these years? What would it do to her marriage? She had been right about Eoin. He had been the best father in the world and still was. She could not have asked for more from a Daddy for Conor and Marie. He was a great husband too. She had hoped to take this secret to the grave, but she had never considered, all those years ago, that she would be up against DNA testing and the World Wide Web. She was beginning to drown in the stress of it all and had no one to turn to. She didn't even know what was right and wrong anymore. Which way was up, or which way was down. She may as well just roll the dice and see what happens, just like nearly four decades ago when Simon had rolled the dice on her and their unborn child.

Chapter Twelve

Conor said goodbye to his family. They had
decided to all come along on the ride to the
airport. It seemed fitting to go together as a
family to see him off after the rollercoaster of the
last two weeks. Myra felt like she was letting
him go all over again, like when he was eighteen
and they had seen him off to university in
England. This time, she did not know if she
would see him again, depending on what his
family search turned up. She held him tight.
Then let him go. Daddy and Marie hugged him
too.

"Take care," called Marie as he started to
walk away.

He turned and gave them one last wave.

Myra, Eoin and Marie left the airport
armin-arm, not saying a word. All lost in their
own thoughts.

Back at home, Conor had a day to himself
before work started again tomorrow. On the
doormat, as he arrived back, was a parcel. He
knew straight away what it was. It was his DNA
testing kit. No time like the present, he thought.
He put his bag down, opened the parcel and
took out the instructions: To take a DNA
sample, open one of the packets containing two
swabs and take out a single swab. Rub and

rotate the swab firmly against the inside of the person's cheek for twenty seconds, making sure to collect the cells and not just the saliva. Repeat this process with the second swab. Washing your hands and brushing and rinsing the mouth before collecting samples will help protect the integrity of the sample collected. Eating, drinking, or smoking thirty minutes before collecting the sample may contaminate or mask the DNA. Place in the free post return envelope. Results will be received in six to eight weeks.

He followed the instructions and placed the sample in the envelope. He put his coat and shoes back on and went straight to the post box.

"Good morning, Henry," said Conor as he arrived at work.

"Good morning, Conor. Did you have a good Christmas?"

"Erm, yes, you know just with the family. Beautiful meal. You?"

"Ah yes, a lovely break. Lots of eating and drinking. Glad to be back to a routine now."

"Yeah, I know what you mean. Lisa about?"

"She's just opening up the museum."

Conor nodded. "I'll head down there then. Thanks."

"No problem," said Henry, nodding back.

Conor found Lisa in the abbey museum. She was turning on the lights in the display cabinets.

"Well, hello," she said when she caught sight of him.

She moved towards him, gave him a hug and asked, "Did you have a nice break? A good Christmas?"

Conor was not quite sure how to reply. Eventually, he said, "I think we need a drink after work if I'm to tell you about my Christmas. If you're free?"

"Yes, of course. Everything okay?"

"No, not really. I found out my daddy isn't my daddy."

Lisa looked stunned. "Forget a drink after work. It's so quiet here this time of year. We've only one group booked in for this afternoon, and Henry can see to anyone else who turns up. Staffroom. Now. Let's get the kettle on."

Conor talked to Lisa as they sat at the small staff table on plastic chairs that resembled the ones he had sat on at school. As he spoke out loud for the first time about what had happened to him over the past two weeks, he could hardly believe it himself.

"What I don't understand," said Lisa, "is why your mammy never told you before."

"Well, she didn't want to upset me, I guess."

"I understand that, but if Simon, your biological dad, was a love of her life, and she even named you after him to honour his memory, then it doesn't make any sense." Conor thought about what Lisa was saying to him. She was right. None of this made a whole lot of sense.

His thoughts were interrupted by Henry knocking on the staffroom door.

"Knock, knock," he said. "We okay in here? It's just there's a group wanting a tour, and a couple have arrived to see the museum." "Okay. We're coming now. Thank you, Henry," said Lisa.

"Okay," he responded.

Lisa leant across the table, patting Simon on the hand reassuringly. "Let's still go for that drink after work."

Conor smiled at her. "Thanks, Lisa."

After work, Conor and Lisa sat at a table in a quiet corner of the Abbey View. Conor had not been back since he left his position as manager. It seemed strange seeing someone else in charge. Laura was the new manager, and she was doing a good job. Conor was quite happy to have handed over the reins to her and just be there as a patron.

"So, what are you going to do then? Lisa asked.

"I've done a DNA test to see if I can find any of Simon's family. Maybe I can meet them and find out about him. If I can't meet him, this is the next best thing." "I guess it is. At least you can learn about him. Find out what he was like." "I already know he was the groundskeeper at Dunstan Castle, and he liked music."

"No way," said Lisa. "You're just like him. When do you get the results back?"

"It says six to eight weeks."

"Excuse me," a voice interrupted. "Are you Conor?".

"Hi. Yes, I am."

"Great. I'm Laura, the new manager. It's lovely to meet you. I've heard so much about you from the staff and the customers." "All good, I hope." Conor laughed.

"Ha, yes, mostly." She laughed back. "Music!"

"Music?" Conor was puzzled.

"We need music. We need your music." She pulled out a scrap of paper from her pocket. "You, Sammy, Derek and Aneesha. Everyone keeps asking me when you'll be here."

Conor smiled. Why not, he thought. After the success of their Abbey concert, it was time they had a regular play together, and it might as well be here, entertaining the customers.

"I'll speak to them. See what we can arrange."

"Oh, thank you. That's great. Nice meeting you."

"You too."

She smiled at Lisa as Laura turned back towards the bar.

"Seems nice," says Lisa. "I will definitely be here to hear you guys play."

"I'll message the band now. It will be nice to have something else to focus on while I wait for the results."

***

In the weeks that followed, Conor busied himself with the band and immersed himself in music. He was right; it had been a good distraction. This evening, the band had been asked to play at a special Valentine's event that Laura had organised at the Abbey View. Not something Conor would have organised as manager, but he was happy to go play some music with the others as it was keeping him sane now, waiting for his results. Laura had requested the playlist include some slow romantic numbers but also the usual upbeat

Celtic music. The bar was busy for a winter's evening.

"Hey, Bobby. Nice to see you. Can I get you a drink? Conor approached his friend at the bar.

"Hey there, yourself. Good to see you. How are you keeping?"

"Grand," he answered. "The usual?"

"Yes. It's great seeing you this side of the bar. I'm looking forward to hearing the band." "There you go, sir. Conor moved the pint placed on the bar in front of Bobby. Let's get this show on the road."

The music was fantastic, as always. No wonder they had drawn in such a crowd. Not just couples, either. There were two coach trips and a few groups of friends who had come to enjoy the food and the music. As he sang and played, Conor spotted Sean at the bar. He made a mental note to go say hello and catch up with him after the performance. He really got lost in the music; singing and dancing with his bandmates felt good. As the music came to an end, the patrons clapped and cheered. They shouted more, more. Conor could see Sean was leaving. He wanted to go after him, but Sammy started playing again, and they were off on an encore.

***

It was Monday morning, and Conor had slept in as he was not working today. He heard the post come through the letterbox and jumped out of bed to check if it was the DNA results. It had been over six weeks now since he sent off his sample. He looked at the pile of envelopes. A bill, another bill, and there it was – his DNA results. He opened the envelope and read the letter as quickly as he could and then more carefully to take it all in:

You have no close DNA matches on our database. To find out more, log in to your online account. Once you have taken a test with us, we will update you if anyone who is a DNA match to you joins the database.

He was not sure how to feel. He was hoping for something. If not his Uncle Patrick, perhaps a distant cousin. Maybe Marie had had more luck. Back in Ireland, she was checking for documentation online, at the town hall and the main library in Dublin. He rang her to update her.

"Hi, Conor. What do you know?"

"Hi, Marie. I know these results just came and tell me nothing."

"No matches?"

"No matches."

"How's your search going?"

"Better than yours."

"Really?" Conor sat up straight in his chair.

"Yes. I was just about to ring you, actually. So, I still haven't located Simon's death certificate, but I found a marriage certificate dated 13 July 2003. A Patrick Kelly married Cara Quinn. His parents match the information Mammy gave us. His father, Niall Kelly. His mother, Clodagh Kelly. His age matches, too, thirty-seven in 2003. Makes him fifty-seven today. Three years younger than Simon."

"There's an address?" Conor asks.

"Yes, there's an address, but remember, it's been twenty years nearly, so chances of him still living there are average at best."

"Where? Was he still in Ireland?"

"County Clare. 14 St Bega's Square, County Clare."

"I wonder if that's where they moved after Simon's accident."

"It's just a two-hour drive from here. Thought I'd go at the weekend to see if Patrick still lives there. If you want me to."

"Yes, but what will you say?"

"Well, that's up to you. I can leave it general, say I'm doing some research into a friend's family tree, or I can ask him outright and tell him he has a nephew."

"The first one. Let's find out if it's him first. Then I might book a flight to visit him myself."

***

Marie arrived in County Clare after driving for nearly two hours. She just had to find the right street. *That's it. I'm here,* she said to herself. She drove around the square, past number 14, made a U-turn, then parked up facing the house—a semi-detached with a small garden at the front. She rang Conor. "I'm here," she whispered, but then realised she didn't need to as there was no one about who could hear her.

"What's the plan?" he asked.

"I thought I'd sit here for a while before I go knock on the door. See what I see. Get the lay of the land. I've brought a cuppa with me."

"If you've changed your mind, it's okay, you know. I'll go."

"I've not changed my mind. I just thought if I knocked on the door first and no one answered, I wouldn't have found anything out. I'll just observe while I have my tea, and then I'll go and knock and ring you back afterwards."

"Okay. Thank you, Marie."

"You're welcome. Good luck to us. Okay, catch you later."

"Bye."

Marie poured her cup of tea from her flask. She had the perfect view of the house from here. She could see a spade and some muddy boots by the front door. All the curtains were open. Daffodils were just starting to grow. She looked for more clues. It seemed like a quiet neighbourhood. She saw an elderly couple walking down the street, holding hands. Then she saw a lady at the window and wondered if it was Cara. She looked about the right age. Marie wondered if Cara knew about Conor. Should she knock now or wait to see if she knew if Patrick was home? But at least she knew someone was home. She would give it ten more minutes, finish her tea, then go knock. At the very least, she would be able to talk to Cara.

Five minutes passed, and Marie saw Cara at the window again. She was laughing and smiling, talking to someone. Marie couldn't see who, but this was it. As she walked towards the door, she could hear music playing. She knocked loudly on the door to make sure she was heard above the music. She waited only a moment, and the lady answered the door.

"Hello, can I help you?" she said.

"Oh, hello. Sure, yes, I am hoping so. My name is Marie, and I'm researching my family tree. I wondered if Patrick and Cara Kelly still lived here."

"Yes, I'm Cara and Patrick's inside. Do we know you?"

"Great. No, you don't know me, but I think there's maybe a family link in my ancestry with Patrick's. Did you say he was in? Can I speak to him?"

"Patrick!" Cara shouted.

Patrick appeared at the door.

"Now, this young lady is doing some family research and thinks there may be a connection between your family and hers."

"Ah, really. Not that I know of."

"Are your parents Niall Kelly and Clodagh Kelly?"

"Yes, that was Mammy and Daddy. What's the connection?"

"I'm not sure yet," said Marie. "Did you have a brother called Simon?"

"Erm, it's been nice meeting you, but we're very busy now."

"I'm sorry, have I upset you? I know your brother passed away."

"Not my brother," he said and closed the door.

Marie headed back to her car to ring Conor, trying to digest what had just happened. It was good news, she supposed. She had found them, but why did he not want to answer the questions about Simon, and what did he mean by "not my brother"?

Marie took her phone out to ring Conor when it started ringing in her hand. It was Daddy.

"Marie."

"Yes, Daddy."

"It's Mammy. She's in the hospital. They took her in an ambulance. They said it was a heart attack."

Marie put her hand over her mouth and breathed slowly to calm her panic.

"I'm here now. Where are you? Can you come?"

"I'm out of town, Daddy, but I'll get there as soon as I can. I'm in the car now." She started the engine. "It's going to take me two hours. I'll put my phone on hands-free. Ring me as soon as you know anything."

"Okay, Marie, I will. Drive safe, please."

"I will, Daddy. Bye."

Marie did drive as safely as she could, but she drove fast. Faster than she maybe should have done. When she arrived at the hospital, she dashed straight in to find Mammy and Daddy.

"Myra Murphy," she said to the nurse at reception. "My Mammy, she's had a heart attack." Then Daddy appeared.

"Daddy." He put his arm around her. He was visibly shaken. She's this way, darling. She's going to be okay the doctors are saying. She has to stay in a week or so for monitoring. They're going to talk to us again soon to tell us more.
She's sleeping right now."

Marie's phone started ringing. "It's Conor," she said to Daddy.

"I haven't told him yet," said Daddy.

"I'll tell him. I'll be back." She wandered down the corridor back to the entrance.

"Hello?"

"Hi, Marie. It's been over two hours. I couldn't wait any longer for you to ring me. Was he there? Did you meet him?"

"Listen, Conor. I'm at the hospital, it's Mammy. She's had a heart attack."

Silence

"Conor, are you still there?"

"Yes. Jesus, is she going to be okay?"

"I haven't seen her yet, but the doctors have told Daddy she's okay and resting. I've just arrived, so I'll ring you back when I have more information."

"Okay, Marie."

163

"I better go. Talk soon."

"Bye."

Marie went back to Daddy. He looked tired.

"Is she still sleeping?"

"Yes." He nodded.

"Maybe I could get you something to eat."

"Oh no, I couldn't eat."

"A drink then."

"Yes. Go on, then. Don't be long, though. I want you to be here when the doctor comes back."

"Okay, Daddy, I won't be long."

Later, Marie rang Conor back.

"Conor, Conor, can you hear me? Where are you?"

"Yes, Marie, I can hear you. I'm at the airport. My flight leaves in half an hour."

"What? You're on your way?"

"Well, yes, I couldn't just sit there waiting for news. So, I rang Lisa to take some time off and then booked the next available flight. What have the doctors said?"

"She has very high blood pressure. She needs to take medication, and they've suggested cutting out alcohol and stress. She needs to relax and take it easy."

"Stress? Stress has caused it?"

"Well, it's contributed to it. She hadn't been taking her blood pressure tablets."

"Listen, that's me. I'm boarding."

"Should I pick you up from the airport?"

"You stay with Daddy. I'll make my own way there. Okay, bye. See you soon."

"Bye, safe journey."

It was late in the evening when Conor arrived at the hospital. Visiting time was coming to an end, but he was allowed in for a short time.

Mammy was awake. Marie and Daddy were sitting on chairs next to her bedside. He quietly joined them. He gave Mammy a kiss on her forehead and then sat down next to Marie. "How are you feeling, Mammy?" "Tired," she said.

"Yes, we'll be going and let you get some more sleep. Get rested up."

"You'll come back in the morning, though, Eoin."

"Yes, of course, my love," Eoin reassured Myra.

"Mammy, I'll help Daddy pack all your things. I've got the list I made earlier. Was there anything else you needed?"

"No. I don't think so," replied Mammy.

"Mammy," Conor said, holding her hand,

"I don't want you to worry. I love you just as much now as I have ever done. Nothing has changed. I don't blame you. You did the best you could. I don't know what I'd do without you."

She gently squeezed his hand, too tired to talk.

"Come on now," said Daddy. "Let's let her rest."

"Okay," said Conor. "Bye, Mammy."

"Bye, Mammy, love you," said Marie.

Daddy said goodbye last. He bent down and whispered in Myra's ear. "Goodnight, my love. Sleep well. I'll miss you tonight. See you in the morning."

With that, she was asleep, and he crept out quietly.

Marie drove them all back to Mammy and Daddy's house. She and Daddy packed a bag to take in the morning with all Mammy's things on the list. Then, when Daddy had gone off to bed, Marie and Conor sat down to talk.

"It's my fault," said Conor.

"Don't be ridiculous," said Marie. "Yes, Mammy has been stressed and not herself. That's understandable considering everything that she's told us. But you didn't ask for this to happen, and you certainly didn't cause it."

"Did you tell Daddy where you were today?"

"No, I didn't tell him."

"I don't think we should tell Daddy or Mammy now. I don't want to cause her any more stress."

"But I found him," Marie said. "Patrick, he was there."

"What did he say?"

"Not too much, to be honest. He confirmed who he and his wife were. Then I asked about his mother and father, which was all confirmed, so I asked about his brother, Simon. And that's when he said he was busy and sent me on my way."

"He didn't say anything about Simon?"

"Well, he did say something a bit strange."

"What?"

"Something like my brother's not dead. Maybe there's a third brother we don't know about?"

"Maybe. Still, as it's caused Mammy lots of stress, I'll leave it be. For now, this family, my family, needs me. And I need you. Nothing else matters."

***

167

When Mammy came home a week later, Conor had made up her room with fresh bedding and a chocolate on her pillow. He had bought her a new dressing gown and slippers, just like she had done for him. Marie had batch cooked enough to feed the entire neighbourhood for a month and put it in the freezer for Mammy and Daddy. Daddy had cut Mammy some beautiful daffodils from the garden and put them in a vase next to her favourite sitting chair to brighten the place up. "Bring the outside in for her after spending a week in hospital."

Mammy was very quiet when she came home. Conor hoped he had reassured her enough in the hospital to relieve her of some of her stress and worry, but she seemed distant. He hated leaving her this way, but he had been there nearly two weeks and had to get home and back to work. Marie dropped him off at the airport.

"Ring me if you need me. If anything changes with Mammy's health."

"I will. I promise."

Conor hugged Marie goodbye. "Take care. See you soon."

"Bye, Conor."

Chapter Thirteen

Conor and Lisa had gone for a drink after work at the Abbey View.

"So, your mum's doing okay?"

"Yes, the doctor's saying everything is good physically, and she's taking all her medication."

"But …" said Lisa.

"Marie says she's not left the house. Daddy keeps asking if she wants to go out for lunch or a walk to get a bit of sun, but she just sits in her chair. It's just not like Mammy. It's like she's had a mental breakdown or something."

"Maybe the shock of the heart attack?"

"Maybe. But I think there's more to it."

"You mean your father?"

"Yes. I think there must be more she isn't telling me. Like there's still some heavy weight on her mind."

"Try not to worry, love. She's in good hands with Marie and your Daddy, by the sounds of it. Listen, I've got to get off. See you tomorrow?"

"Yes, I'll have one more and be off soon too. See you tomorrow."

Lisa put on her jacket, placed a sympathetic hand on Conor's shoulder and said goodnight.

Conor went to the bar to order a drink. "Same again, please, Laura," he said.

She smiled. "Coming right up." She looked very happy in her role. Conor had been in such a deep conversation with Lisa that he hadn't noticed Sean in his usual quiet spot.

Sean approached him. "So, what do you know?"

Laura brought Conor's pint over.

"Let me get that for you," said Sean.

"Thanks a million," replied Conor.

"Has your friend gone?"

"Lisa? Yes."

"Can I join you, then?"

"Yeah, sure. It will be nice to catch up, mate."

Sean joined Conor at the table where he had been sitting with Lisa.

"So, is that Lisa from the abbey? I hear you work there now. Are you liking it?"

"Yes, Lisa works with me at the abbey. And, yes, I am enjoying it."

"Haven't seen you in here much recently."

"Well, no, I gave it a break when I left. And I've been over in Ireland this last couple of weeks."

"Back in Dunstan?"

"Yes. Mammy took ill."

"I'm sorry to hear that. Will she be okay?" He seemed genuinely concerned.

"She had a heart attack, but she's home now."

"But you're still worried about her?"

"Yeah, she's had a lot of stress on her."

"Ah well, yes, stress is the worst on your health. Sure, I know that for a fact. Is it anything you can help with?"

"I tried."

There was a silent pause. Sean did not reply as he was not sure Conor had finished speaking. Conor continued.

"I've been looking for my biological father's family."

"Really?"

"Yes, but I don't want to put any stress on Mammy. It's hard for her, reliving the past."

"But she told you all about your biological father, and you've been wanting to find his family?"

"Yes."

"Your Mammy told you everything about him? What happened?"

"Yes, my sister, Marie, found my Uncle Patrick."

"She found Patrick?"

"Yes, but it was the day Mammy got taken to the hospital, so I haven't got any closer to knowing my biological father."

"I never did tell you whereabouts in Ireland I grew up, did I now?" said Sean.

"No, I don't recall that you did."

"I grew up in Dunstan."

"Really? You've never told me that before."

"No, I haven't. Yes, I lived there with my Daddy, Mammy and my younger brother."

"Oh yes, you did mention you had a younger sibling. Well, my biological father used to work at Dunstan Castle."

"He was the groundskeeper," said Sean.

"Ye-e-s," said Conor, looking confused. "You knew him?"

"Yes. I still do."

"What do you mean?" The conversation had taken a turn that neither had expected this evening.

"I've been wanting to tell you for the past five years since I arrived in James Bridge. Look, my hands are shaking."

"Sean, you're not making any sense," said Conor firmly.

"I know, I'm not doing this very well. II'm— Let me introduce myself to you again properly this time. He put out his hand for Conor to shake. I'm Simon Sean Kelly."

Conor limply took his hand and then let go still not understanding what Sean was saying to him.

"I'm your father."

Conor turned pale. He was literally staring at a ghost. He couldn't speak. He was frozen to the spot, like his brain had shut down all non-essential functions while it worked out what was going on here.

"Conor. Conor. Did you hear me?" asked Sean.

Eventually, Conor spoke. "You can't be my father. My father is dead."

"What? I'm not. I'm here. I thought you said you were looking for me."

"I was. Well, your family anyway. To find out about you. I mean him."

"Me," said Sean. "You've found me. Why did you think I was dead? Did Patrick tell you that? We fell out when I went to prison."

"Prison?"

"Yes, but your mammy would have told you all about that, I suppose. That's why I never introduced myself properly before. I just assumed you wouldn't want to know me. I just wanted to get to know my son. That's why I moved here."

"Just wait a minute. This is too much. I'm sure you must be mistaken, Sean. My mammy told me my father had died in a road accident before I was born.

"Oh, alright. She did? I see. Right then. So, you didn't want to know me. I'm sorry, I've made a big mistake." And with that, Sean stood up to leave.

Conor was left in stunned silence. After a minute, he turned and called out. "Wait!" But it was too late. Sean had already left.

Conor sat there a while, trying to process everything he had just heard. I need to speak to Sean, he thought to himself. Then he remembered a conversation they had a while ago and knew where to find him.

Conor found Sean sitting on the grass in the abbey cloister. He was leaning against the wall.

"Sean," he called, "let's finish talking."

"Okay. How did you know I'd be here?"

"You once told me the abbey reminded you of a place you had spent a lot of time. It takes you back to a happy time. Is that place Dunstan Castle, where you were groundskeeper?"

"Yes. Your mammy told you that?"

"Yes, she did."

"You believe me?"

"I'm starting to. I need you to tell me why Mammy told me you had died in a road accident."

"I can't," Sean said. He now seemed to be withdrawing from this conversation with Conor.

"Can't or won't?"

"Ask your Mammy," he said coldly.

"I'm asking you, Sean."

"I don't know why she told you I was dead. Dead to her, maybe."

"What does that mean, Sean?" Conor was getting frustrated.

Sean stood up to leave.

"If you are my father, you will tell me," Conor shouted.

Sean turned back to face Conor. "I killed someone," he shouted back.

"You-you killed someone?"

"Yes."

"What happened? Was it an accident?"

"No, son, it was not an accident. I murdered a man. I purposefully targeted him. Aimed a stolen car at him. And after I had sent him up over the bonnet, his body smashed onto the road. I turned and saw your mammy was watching me, and I did not care. I put the car in

175

reverse and backed up over the body. I can't even blame Patrick. Sure, it was his mess. He'd come out of prison and straight back to his old ways. He owed money to the wrong people. But I enjoyed it. I wanted to do it. I didn't know Myra was pregnant, but it would not have made a difference to me. I would still have done it." He looked at Conor with wild eyes—such anger and bitterness.

"You're not my father," said Conor. "You are nothing to me. You don't deserve to be my father. Why did you come to James Bridge?"

"Curiosity. I wanted to know what my son was like. If he'd made anything of himself. My family didn't want anything to do with me. Even Patrick turned his back on me. Apparently, he's turned his life around and even got married."

"You should leave."

"Okay, just give me a couple of grand to set myself up, and I'll go."

"Yeah."

"Yeah, you will?"

"Yeah, that just confirms it. The type of man you are. That's why you wanted to see what I'd made of myself, is it? Bet you were really disappointed when I left my manager position, weren't you? You couldn't get your free pints and food anymore. And to think I felt sorry for you being on your own."

"Just a grand, then."

"No, you're getting nothing. You deserve nothing. You don't know what it means to be a father." And Conor left.

Chapter Fourteen

Conor had a few days off coming up and was
booking his flight to Ireland to see his family,
particularly how his mammy was getting on. It
had been several weeks since he had seen Sean.
He was glad. He did not want to see him again.
He found it quite disturbing now, knowing that
Sean had been watching him over the past five
years, pretending to be a mate.

Conor had looked up Patrick's number
and rang him. He had been shocked at first but
spoke to him to confirm everything, including
the fact that when Sean had got out of prison, he
had borrowed money from him and drank and
gambled it all away. He also talked about how
he had tried to support Sean mainly out of guilt
that he had drawn him into a bad situation all
those years ago, but he wanted more and more
money and started stealing from Patrick. Conor
explained that he was grateful that Patrick had
agreed to speak to him but that it would not be
possible to have a relationship with him in the
future and that he would prefer it if he did not
tell anyone they had spoken. He had said he did
not want to upset his family, and Patrick agreed,
wishing him all the best.

Marie picked Conor up from the airport.
He felt bad not telling her about meeting his

biological father and about his contact with Patrick after everything she had done for him recently. However, this was between him and Mammy. He did not want his mammy to suffer anymore because of someone else's mistakes, and if that meant it would forever be between the two of them, then that's the way it would be. Mammy deserved a loving marriage — a happy family. He would find the right moment to tell her he knew and that he was okay, and he loved her more than ever. Marie filled Conor in on Mammy's health since she had left the hospital.

"The doctors are happy with her physically, but she seems so down. She hasn't been outside for weeks, and she'll only eat dry crackers," explained Marie. "Maybe you might have some luck."

"I hope so," Conor said.

When they arrived at Mammy and Daddy's, it was very quiet. There were no neighbours around eating cakes and drinking tea. There was no chatting or laughter. Mammy sat in her armchair in the back room, reading. Daddy had moved his comfy chair in from the front sitting room and sat next to her, reading his paper.

"Hello, Mammy. Hello, Daddy," said Conor. He put his bags down and went and gave Mammy a kiss on her forehead. She smiled, which was nice to see. Marie put the

179

kettle on. Conor perched on the arm of Mammy's chair and placed his arm around her. It was funny; he felt like a little boy again, needing his Mammy, but he also felt very grown up and protective of her. He told her all about his flight and how he had sat next to a couple from Dublin who had just been to a wedding in Yorkshire. Then, he talked about the mild turbulence they had experienced that had not lasted very long.

Later, Conor suggested that Marie take Daddy out for a bite to eat and a walk to the duck pond. As Daddy had been keeping Mammy company, he had not been out much himself.

"I'll stay and keep Mammy company. You two enjoy yourselves." Daddy was quite pleased about the suggestion and went to put a nice shirt on.

Thank you, Marie mouthed over to Conor.

"Sure, we'll have a grand time, won't we, Mammy?" he said, trying to make her laugh.

When Marie and Daddy had gone, Conor asked mammy to come outside.

"No, I'm happy here," Mammy replied.

"Well, you're not really, are you? I'm sorry, but on this occasion, I can't take no for an answer. Mammy, I need you outside." And he took her hands.

"Okay. Just for five minutes," she said.

They sat on the deck chairs in the garden. The grass was a little overgrown as Daddy had not had time to tend to the garden. Conor made a mental note that he would get the lawnmower out tomorrow and cut it. "It's a beautiful September day, Mammy. Nice and warm and sunny. Makes up for all that rain we had in August. You don't like September very much, do you, Mammy?

"No, I don't suppose I do." She looked at him, surprised that he knew this.

"I think I would feel the same." He paused for a moment and then continued. "I know, Mammy." "Know what?" she asked.

"I know everything. I know why you don't like September and why you kept the secret about my daddy. I know why his family moved away."

"You do? What is it you think you know?"

He wouldn't tell Mammy he had met Simon, but he would tell her about speaking to Patrick. "I found Patrick."

"Patrick Kelly?"

"Yes, Simon's brother. I know he's not dead, Mammy. I know what he did. That he's a murderer. That he killed someone, and you had to watch. I'm so sorry that happened to you." Mammy started to cry.

"It's okay, Mammy, you let it out."

"I'm so sorry I lied," she said through sobs.

"Don't you dare be sorry, Mammy. You didn't lie, I know that now. You just kept the truth to yourself to protect me, and now I'm going to keep the truth to myself to protect you."

"I can't ask you to do that."

"You're not asking me, Mammy. I'm telling you. I don't want this to destroy our family. You, me, Daddy Marie. We are all good people. We all love each other. We cannot let this man ruin our lives over his mistake. If I'd discovered this earlier, I might not have understood, but at this point in my life, I do. We matter. Now matters, not the past."

"But I lied to Daddy too."

"Yes, and I understand why you did it, Mammy. You gave me the best daddy in the world. He treated me completely as his own and still does. We need to make a pact right now. We will leave the past in the past and start enjoying life again. We will love Daddy and Marie and each other. We will all look after each other. If you give up now, Mammy, you may as well have not been strong your whole life. I need you now more than ever. You made the decision for both of us when I was a baby. Now, I'm making the decision for both of us. I don't want Daddy and Marie to know, and I don't want anything to do with Simon or Patrick. I already told Patrick so."

Mammy wiped her eyes.

"Now, I'm making you something to eat, and you'll eat it, will you?" "Yes." She nodded.

"Then we'll go for a walk?"
"Yes." She smiled and nodded again.

***

When Daddy and Marie got home, Conor and Mammy were playing cards. They'd invited Carol over to play too. The house was full of laughter.

"This is nice," said Marie.

"Hello, Carol. Nice to see you," said Daddy.

"Come and join us," said Mammy.

"Okay, deal us in."

It was such a great evening. Conor felt content and happy. It was the best thing, just playing cards with his family and neighbour. He would have never appreciated it before, but now it was like magic, and he wished he could bottle the moment.

After Mammy and Daddy had gone to bed and Carol had gone home, Marie told Conor, "I don't know what you said to Mammy while we were out but thank you."

"We had a really good chat. I made Mammy something to eat, then we walked to the duck pond, and I took her for an ice cream. We sat on the bench, and I told her some jokes. When we got home, we knocked on Carol's door to see if she wanted to play cards. She was so pleased to see Mammy."

"That's fantastic. It's like a weight has been lifted," said Marie.

"It certainly is," replied Conor.

"I just hope it continues."

"I have a feeling it will."

Printed in Great Britain
by Amazon

40820124R00106